The Search for Cindy Austin

Nancy searched the bright red cattle barn thoroughly, but there was no sign of Cindy.

Nancy stepped back outside, her gaze sweeping the area. She walked along the edge of the electric fence. There was nowhere Cindy could be.

As she retraced her steps, Nancy heard a scrunching noise behind her, and strong hands suddenly pushed her to her knees. Turning, she caught sight of a pair of black rubber boots and dark slacks.

"Hey—!"

Before she could say anything else, the hands picked her up and pushed her—directly toward the humming wires of the electric fence!

Nancy Drew
Mystery Stories

#57 The Triple Hoax
#58 The Flying Saucer Mystery
#59 The Secret in the Old Lace
#60 The Greek Symbol Mystery
#61 The Swami's Ring
#62 The Kachina Doll Mystery
#63 The Twin Dilemma
#64 Captive Witness
#65 Mystery of the Winged Lion
#66 Race Against Time
#67 The Sinister Omen
#68 The Elusive Heiress
#69 Clue in the Ancient Disguise
#70 The Broken Anchor
#71 The Silver Cobweb
#72 The Haunted Carousel
#73 Enemy Match
#74 The Mysterious Image
#75 The Emerald-eyed Cat Mystery
#76 The Eskimo's Secret
#77 The Bluebeard Room
#78 The Phantom of Venice
#79 The Double Horror of Fenley Place
#80 The Case of the Disappearing Diamonds
#81 The Mardi Gras Mystery
#82 The Clue in the Camera
#83 The Case of the Vanishing Veil
#84 The Joker's Revenge
#85 The Secret of Shady Glen
#86 The Mystery of Misty Canyon
#87 The Case of the Rising Stars
#88 The Search for Cindy Austin
#89 The Case of the Disappearing Deejay
#90 The Puzzle at Pineview School
#91 The Girl Who Couldn't Remember
#92 The Ghost of Craven Cove
#93 The Case of the Safecracker's Secret
#94 The Picture-Perfect Mystery

Available from MINSTREL Books

NANCY DREW MYSTERY STORIES®

88

NANCY DREW®

THE SEARCH FOR CINDY AUSTIN

CAROLYN KEENE

A MINSTREL® BOOK

PUBLISHED BY POCKET BOOKS

New York   London   Toronto   Sydney   Tokyo   Singapore

A MINSTREL PAPERBACK *ORIGINAL*

 A Minstrel Book published by
POCKET BOOKS, a division of Simon & Schuster Inc.
1230 Avenue of the Americas, New York, NY 10020

ISBN: 0-671-66313-5

First Minstrel Books printing April 1989

10 9 8 7 6 5 4 3 2

Contents

1   *Child Genius*   1
2   *The Search Is On*   10
3   *A Shocking Discovery*   20
4   *Detour*   27
5   *Death Squeeze*   35
6   *Shadowy Figure*   48
7   *"So We Meet Again . . ."*   61
8   *A Dangerous Game*   68
9   *Kidnapped!*   77
10   *Secret Formula*   87
11   *Abandoned Mill*   98
12   *Trapped!*   104
13   *Turning the Tables*   114
14   *The Master*   124
15   *Touchdown*   136

THE SEARCH FOR
CINDY AUSTIN

1

Child Genius

"So you're the famous girl detective," Cindy Austin said loudly, deliberately stopping the hum of conversation around the dinner table.

Nancy Drew looked up, surprised. Her blue eyes examined the twelve-year-old girl who sat across the table from her. Cindy hadn't spoken a word since they'd all sat down to dinner. In fact, her silence had prompted Cindy's mother, Dr. Barbara Austin, to try and prod her into conversation.

"Well, I don't know how famous I am," Nancy answered, smiling. "But I have solved a few cases."

"Oh, but you're really famous!" Julianne Connelly put in excitedly. At eleven, Julianne was only a year younger than her cousin, Cindy, but unlike Cindy, Julianne had chattered on about

1

her friends and her school all through the meal. "Everybody in River Heights knows about you. That last case you solved was in all the papers. Mom said so."

Julianne's mother, Katherine Connelly, smiled. Katherine was a lawyer who worked with Nancy's father, Carson Drew, at his law firm. A widow, she'd known the Drews for several years.

When Katherine had learned that her sister, Dr. Barbara Austin, and Barbara's husband, Dr. Terence Austin, were coming for a visit, she had invited Nancy and her father to dinner. The Austins were celebrated research scientists who had just finished a special project for the United States government. Katherine had explained that the project was top-secret until the Austins could present their findings at a special meeting of the World Health Organization at the United Nations.

Turning to Cindy, Katherine remarked, "Nancy's reputation as a detective is well-known throughout the area."

Cindy kept her eyes on Nancy. "Well, then, how do you solve your cases?" she asked, tossing her straight brown hair. "Do you use computers? I bet you know a lot of detectives on the police force. Do they help you? Have you studied the criminal mind?"

"Cindy," Barbara Austin broke in uncomfortably. "Give Nancy a chance to answer."

"Well, I——" Nancy started.

"You're not one of those people who relies on instinct, are you? I can't believe that's how you would work," Cindy interrupted.

Nancy was momentarily speechless. Though Nancy's father had mentioned Cindy was a child genius, Nancy hadn't quite expected her to talk like an exasperated adult. Cindy looked older than twelve, too, despite her uncombed hair and obvious indifference to her appearance. Her chin was sharp and determined, and she stared at Nancy with deep suspicion.

"Cindy," Dr. Terence Austin said sternly, "Nancy and her father were invited to dinner at your aunt's house in order to meet all of us. This is not an inquisition."

Cindy set her jaw and looked down at her plate. Nancy couldn't help feeling sorry for her. Unlike Julianne, Cindy seemed to say and do just the wrong thing.

When she glanced back up, her chin was trembling a bit from emotion. "I've got an intelligence quotient over a hundred and sixty," she said.

Julianne looked at her cousin with awe. "That means you're a genius," she said. "Mom said so."

"With an IQ like that you must be a whiz in the classroom," Nancy remarked.

"Classroom." Cindy sniffed. "I have private tutors."

An uncomfortable silence fell over the table, and Katherine Connelly said quickly, "Would anyone like dessert?"

There were murmurs of agreement all around. Even Cindy seemed embarrassed, but she demanded loudly of Nancy, "So how *do* you solve your cases?"

Tucking a strand of reddish blond hair behind her ear, Nancy said politely, "Well, I try to examine the facts and draw logical conclusions. And every once in a while I even play a hunch."

"That's not very scientific."

"No," Nancy agreed, "but sometimes it works."

"Really." Cindy was unimpressed. "It can't be that hard to be a detective. I imagine I could be a good one if I tried. Probably as good as you."

At that moment Katherine hurried back carrying a tray covered with plates of cream-filled chocolate cake. Wondering why Cindy had chosen to attack her, Nancy accepted her plate and turned her attention toward the conversation her father was having with Terence Austin.

"I understand Katherine works at your office," Terence was saying to Nancy's father.

"We've been known to put our heads together over a tough case or two." The famed criminal lawyer smiled at Katherine. "She's one of the best attorneys in town."

"Hear, hear!" Katherine laughed. "This is

turning into a mutual admiration society. I'm so glad you all had a chance to meet."

"Me, too." Terence sighed and leaned back in his chair. "It's nice to take a break. It's been a long, hard, exciting project and I, for one, will be glad when it's finally over." He glanced through the dining room doors. Nancy followed his gaze to the three security people who were the Austins' constant companions.

Security and secrecy, Nancy thought. This must be some project!

"Well, I'll be glad when it's all over, too," Cindy declared. "I'm tired of moving around, and I don't like Washington, D.C., any more than I liked New York City." Tossing her napkin on her plate, she scraped back her chair and added disdainfully, "And River Heights is a drag."

She stomped out of the room and Barbara sighed unhappily. "This has been hard on Cindy," she said so quietly that Nancy could barely hear her.

"May I be excused?" Julianne asked her mother, and when Katherine nodded, she hurried after Cindy.

"I wish Cindy would try to get along with people," Terence muttered. "She's making the worst out of a bad situation."

"It's hard for her." Barbara was quick to her daughter's defense. "Intellectually, she's way ahead of children her age, but emotionally, she's still a twelve-year-old. She doesn't know how to act. The way she challenged you, Nancy, well"— Barbara shrugged helplessly—"it's really her way of getting to know you."

Seeing how upset Barbara was, Nancy said, "Why don't I go see what Cindy's doing?" Though she found Cindy's attitude somewhat annoying, she could see how awkward and lonely the girl felt. Maybe Cindy just needed a friend.

"Leave her for a while," Terence said with a shake of his head. "She can't always depend on people's sympathy. Especially mine. After the last few stunts she's pulled, I've lost patience with her."

"What sort of stunts?" Nancy asked.

"When we first moved to Washington, D.C., she ran away a few times, just for a couple of hours," Barbara explained. "It scared us and almost drove Tyler crazy."

"Tyler?" Nancy asked.

"Tyler Scott, the head of our security team," Terence explained, his gaze once more turning to the people waiting outside the room. "He and his men, John Wiggins and Ray Katz, keep an eye on things. Tyler's staying in one of Katherine's guest rooms. Wiggins and Katz are at the Riverside Inn, but they spend most of their time here with us."

"Your project must be very important for you to need a full-time security team," Carson noted.

"Yes, well, I wish I could tell you more about it, but we must keep security as tight as possible."

The discussion turned more general and Nancy slipped away from the table. It had been a while since Cindy had taken off and Nancy wanted to make sure she talked to the girl before leaving the Connellys'.

Unable to find Cindy on the main floor, Nancy mounted the stairs to the second story. At the landing she paused, glancing both ways down the white-paneled hallway. "Cindy?" she called.

"She's not up here," said Julianne, appearing in the open doorway of the room at the end of the hall.

"Are you sure? She's not downstairs."

Julianne bit her lower lip. "I haven't seen her."

"Which one's her room?"

"That one." Julianne pointed to a closed door halfway down the hall. "I knocked on it when I came upstairs. She didn't answer, but she could be in there. She likes to be alone a lot."

Nancy wasn't surprised that Cindy had trouble making friends. Julianne was practically begging for her cousin's attention, but Cindy obviously hadn't even met her halfway.

Knocking on Cindy's door, Nancy called, "Cindy?"

There was no answer.

"Cindy?" Nancy called again. When there was still no answer she twisted the knob and stuck her head inside. She drew in a sharp breath. The room was a mess! Drawers were thrown open, and clothes were tossed all over the place. The window on the far wall was open, and the curtains were fluttering in the stiff October breeze.

Nancy quickly crossed the room and shut the window, shivering from the chill. She looked around, perplexed. Had Cindy thrown all her clothes from the drawers in a fit of anger? Where was she?

"Cindy?" Barbara Austin's voice sounded from the hallway. Before Nancy could explain that Cindy wasn't in her room, Barbara appeared in the doorway. "What is this? Where's Cindy?"

"I'm not sure. I found the room like this, but she isn't here."

"She's not downstairs," Barbara said quickly. "I looked for her. That's why I came up here. Where is she?" she asked, her voice rising. "Where did she go?"

Nancy turned back toward the window and threw open the sash, sweeping her gaze over the shingled rooftop. On this side of the house the roofline sloped gently down almost the full two stories. It would be easy enough for an agile twelve-year-old to slide to the ground if she wanted to. Nancy could almost make out twin tracks on the shingles, as if Cindy's shoes had swept a path through the pine needles and moss scattered on the rooftop.

"I think," Nancy said slowly, "that Cindy may have climbed down from the roof."

"Oh no! She wouldn't run away again!" Barbara Austin's voice shook.

Before Nancy could answer, Barbara clasped Nancy's arm in a tight grip. "Something's happened," she said hoarsely. "Cindy wouldn't leave on her own again. She wouldn't!"

"What makes you so certain that—"

Barbara's fingers dug into Nancy's arm. "Cindy gave me her solemn word that she wouldn't run away again," she said, the intensity of her voice sending a shiver up Nancy's spine. "This time she's been kidnapped!"

2

The Search Is On

"Kidnapped?" Nancy echoed in disbelief. "Why do you think she's been kidnapped?" She pointed out the window. "Those must be Cindy's tracks on the roof, and if they are, she must have left on her own."

Barbara Austin's hand was now over her mouth and her eyes were wide with terror. Given Cindy's history of running away, Nancy was puzzled by Barbara's attitude. "What tracks?" Barbara asked.

"There are marks on the roof," Nancy told her. "It looks like Cindy slid to the ground. This window was open when I came in. I only shut it to keep out the cold."

"Really?" Barbara swept past Nancy and stared out at the roof. "You're right!" she said with relief. "Oh, you're right. There *are* tracks. Thank goodness! After I heard about Tyler seeing that man outside the lab . . ."

Her voice trailed off, but Nancy asked, "What man?"

"Oh, nothing." With a shaky laugh Barbara said, "Never mind. It's something I can't talk about. I've just been doubly concerned about Cindy lately and that's why I made her promise she wouldn't run off again. I was sure she wouldn't break her promise." She sighed. "But it looks as if she has."

"What's happened?" Terence walked into the bedroom and surveyed the mess. "What's all this? Where's Cindy?"

"We're not sure," Barbara said, and as she told him about Cindy's disappearance, her husband's face flushed.

"What is she thinking of?" he muttered through his teeth. "Where's Tyler? I want him to find her right now!"

The security men were summoned to the living room, and when they entered, Nancy got her first clear look at them. As Terence Austin began telling Tyler Scott about Cindy's disappearance, Nancy studied Scott. He must be somewhere in his thirties, she thought, and he has a mean, tough look about him. Nancy wondered how Cindy would dare go against his orders. The other two men, Wiggins and Katz, had Tyler's

11

same look and build, too. Their resemblance made Nancy wonder if all security people came from the same mold.

"I'll find her," Tyler said reassuringly. "If she's taken off on her own, she won't be far." He turned to Barbara. "What was she wearing?"

"Just jeans and a T-shirt. She must have taken her jacket. The only one we brought is navy blue."

Tyler nodded, then, barking orders at the other two security men, strode through the front door.

Nancy turned to Terence Austin. "Dr. Austin, each time Cindy's left before, how long has she stayed away?"

"Cindy's only been gone a few hours at a time." He ran a hand through his hair in exasperation. "Although once it was overnight."

"You don't actually think she would stay out all night again?" Barbara asked, alarmed.

"Barbara, I really don't know what she'll do next!"

Nerves were stretched to breaking, so Nancy tried to be positive. "Why don't we talk to Julianne?" she suggested. "If Cindy planned to run away, she might have said something earlier today."

"Good idea," Carson Drew agreed. "Terence, you and I will check with Julianne. Nancy, maybe you could go over Cindy's room with Barbara and Katherine."

"There might be some clue we've overlooked,"

Nancy answered with a nod. She knew her father was trying to soothe both of Cindy's parents. "You never know," she added. "She might just be hiding outside and Tyler Scott will find her."

Nancy, Barbara, and Katherine trekked back up to Cindy's room. Barbara picked up one of her daughter's sweaters. "What could have possessed her?" she murmured unhappily. "She knows I don't want her wandering around alone. Especially now, when we're about to make our research known."

Katherine put her arm around her sister's shoulders. "Why don't you let Nancy help you?" she suggested. "Nancy's helped her father out lots of times."

"That's right. You're a detective," Barbara said to Nancy.

Taking her cue from Katherine, Nancy asked, "Is there anywhere in River Heights Cindy might head for? A particular place she likes?"

Barbara shook her head. "We've only been here a few days, and Tyler doesn't want us to go out in public too often. He says our enemies are everywhere, but I hate to believe that."

"Does he mean enemies of the government?" Nancy asked carefully.

"Yes. Unfortunately, news of our project leaked out even though we worked in a top-secret laboratory. There are enemy agents who would kill to get their hands on our research, Nancy. But no one knows we're in River Heights. No one."

13

"Then I imagine Cindy's safe," Katherine reassured her.

"Maybe she'll be back in a few hours," Nancy offered hopefully, but she remembered what Barbara had said about a man hanging around outside the Austins' laboratory. She didn't like the sound of that. Could Cindy be in real danger?

"I hope she's all right." Barbara looked frazzled and worried.

Nancy and Katherine bent to help Barbara sort through the mess. Underneath a pile of sweaters Nancy's hand touched a piece of paper. She pulled it out and read the printed message. "A nursery rhyme!" she said in some surprise. "Was this written by Cindy?"

Barbara looked at the handwriting and nodded.

"'Little Miss Moffett sat on a tuffet eating her curds and whey. Along came a spider who sat down beside her and frightened Miss Moffett away,'" Nancy read. "*Muffet* is spelled wrong twice. Cindy wouldn't make that kind of error, would she?"

"No." Barbara shook her head. "Cindy's an excellent speller. She's very particular."

"Then there must be a reason for it. I'd like to keep this, if that's okay."

"Nancy, if it'll help you find Cindy, you can keep everything she's written since we've been here."

So saying, Barbara went over to Cindy's desk

and pulled out a small notebook. She handed it to Nancy. It was filled with drawings, scribbles, and stories. "She's only had the notebook since we got to River Heights," Barbara said with a little smile. "Even I'm still amazed at what an active mind she has."

Nancy put the paper with the rhyme on it into the notebook, and they left the room. When Nancy stepped into the hallway, Katherine Connelly pulled her aside. "I'm glad you're helping Barbara. Cindy may just have run away to be alone for a while, but it'll help Barbara to know we're all looking for her."

"I'll do my best to find Cindy," Nancy promised.

She met her father back in the living room. "Julianne couldn't tell us anything," he told her. "Cindy, it seems, rarely talked to her cousin."

"Where do *you* think Cindy is?"

"I don't know, Nancy. But I hope she's still in the area so that Tyler finds her quickly."

Nancy nodded. "Katherine convinced Barbara to let me help in the search, too. Would you mind going home without me? I'd like to look around some more."

Carson Drew smiled. "How about if I lend a hand if I promise not to get in your way?"

Nancy's blue eyes twinkled. "Promise?"

"Promise," he answered with mock seriousness.

"Okay. Then let's search the grounds for any

clues. I know Tyler Scott and his men have probably been all over this place, but I'd just like to recheck."

"No harm in being thorough," her father answered.

They covered every inch of the house and grounds and came up empty-handed. There were simply no clues to Cindy's disappearance.

As they were leaving, Tyler Scott came in the front door. "We'll keep searching all night if necessary," he said, regarding Nancy with disapproval. Clearly, he resented her involvement. "Oh, by the way, Julianne Connelly's bike is missing. We're fairly certain Cindy took it."

"That means she could travel pretty far," Nancy said, more to herself than Tyler Scott.

"We'll find her," the security man told her flatly. "Go home, Miss Drew. There's nothing you can do."

"What about calling the police?" Nancy asked.

"For security reasons, I would rather wait until tomorrow. I'm certain Cindy will be back by then, anyway."

Nancy left with her father but she felt uneasy. Barbara Austin's words haunted her: *There are enemy agents who would kill to get their hands on our research.*

Slurp, slurp.

George Fayne, watching her cousin Bess finish

16

her chocolate fudge milk shake, said dryly, "You're going to suck a hole right through the bottom of that thing."

Pretty, blond-haired Bess made a face at her dark-haired cousin. Bess and George were about as unlike as two girls could be. Bess, dimpled and fair, was content to dream about boys and hang back from the action whenever she was involved in Nancy's cases; George, slim, athletic, and down-to-earth, was as eager as Nancy to jump in feet first. Both girls were Nancy's best friends.

"Lunch was ages ago. And I've been watching what I eat all day," Bess retorted, turning to Nancy for support. The three of them were seated around a table at a fast-food restaurant.

George snorted. "Watching it pass your lips, you mean."

"These are pretty good," Nancy remarked, and noiselessly sipped her own milk shake. Caught in the middle between her two friends, as happened more often than not, she was playing peacemaker.

"Tell me again about this missing whiz kid," George said, reaching for another french fry. "Cindy—what's her name?"

"Cindy Austin. Her mother was afraid she'd been kidnapped, but now it looks like she took off on her own—on her cousin Julianne Connelly's bike." Nancy sighed, finished her milk shake,

17

and thrust the container aside. "I called the Connellys' this morning. Cindy's still missing. I'm really worried about her." Nancy picked up a french fry, then put it back. "I've been reading Cindy's notebook and trying to figure out if the nursery rhyme is a clue. If it is, I don't know what it means," she continued. "This afternoon I'd like to search the neighborhood around the Connellys'. Even if Tyler Scott's men have already been there, they might have missed something."

"Well, what are we waiting for?" George asked. "You've got us to help you now! Cindy's as good as found!"

"Oh, brother." Bess groaned, but she good-naturedly followed George and Nancy out to Nancy's blue sports car.

Nancy drove toward the Connelly house. The Connellys lived on the outskirts of River Heights in an area of sloping farmland, where the closest neighbors were several acres away. Nancy turned into the driveway of the farmhouse nearest to the Connellys', then nearly jumped out of her skin when a horn blasted.

"There's a car behind us," Bess said nervously. "It just pulled in."

Nancy looked around. Tyler Scott was climbing out of a black sedan behind them. He strode rapidly to Nancy's car and jerked open her door.

"Just what do you think you're doing here, Miss Drew?" he demanded angrily. His scowling face was dark with fury. "Didn't I make myself clear last night? Stay away from this investigation. As far as I'm concerned, you're the reason Cindy Austin is missing!"

3

A Shocking Discovery

"I'm the reason!" Nancy echoed, dismayed.

"I overheard what Cindy said to you at dinner last night," Tyler answered flatly. "She practically challenged you to a game of wits. She thinks she's a better detective than you are."

Nancy stared up at him. "You mean you think she ran away because she wants *me* to find her?"

"I don't know what her reasons were, Miss Drew. But I do know that this job should be left to professionals." He waved his arm in the direction of the farm. "This area's been searched, we've questioned all the Connellys' neighbors, and we're widening our circle. You're wasting your time and mine. My men and I will find Cindy Austin."

Nancy was tempted to point out that he hadn't

found Cindy yet, but said instead, "Then I'm sure you won't mind if I look where you've already searched."

His neck turned dark red. She could see he minded very much. But he muttered, "Be my guest," and slammed back into his car.

"What a bear," Bess said as Tyler Scott left.

"He certainly objects to you looking around," George remarked. "Maybe he's afraid you'll beat him to the punch."

"I wonder if he's right, though, about Cindy," Nancy said thoughtfully. "Maybe this is some kind of dare. That would explain a lot of things."

"Like what?" asked Bess.

"Well, it's pretty clear Cindy left on her own. No kidnapper would have attempted to drag her down that roof. A kidnapper would have found an easier way to snatch her. Besides, the tracks were wrong. And Cindy left that strange nursery rhyme."

"And even though Barbara Austin said Cindy had promised never to leave again," Bess remarked, "if she wanted to prove she was a better detective than the famous Nancy Drew—"

"Cindy wouldn't be able to resist the challenge!" George finished. "It makes sense."

Nancy nodded. "Yes, it does. And if that's true, it makes me want to find Cindy all the more. I'd hate to think something happened to her because she was playing a game with me. Barbara told me

21

a man had been seen hanging around their lab in Washington. She's convinced Cindy could be a kidnapping target."

"She could be in more danger than she knows," George said grimly, voicing Nancy's thoughts.

By late afternoon, they had checked out three homes along the road. But they had found no sign of the missing girl.

"I'm thirsty," Bess complained, as they walked toward the last farmhouse along the road. "The ground's wet and my feet are soaked."

George looked at the cloud-covered sky. "I hope it doesn't rain all week. The River Heights football game against Chatham Central is scheduled for Friday, and even I hate football in the rain."

But Nancy wasn't listening. She was thinking about Cindy. Where had Cindy found shelter? Had she run away because of a dare? Was the notebook a clue? Though Nancy had searched through it the night before, she'd found nothing in the sketches and doodles to indicate where Cindy might have gone.

George knocked on the farmhouse door. A white-haired man opened it and introduced himself as Mr. Carver. Nancy told him they were searching for Cindy Austin.

"Cindy Austin?" he repeated blankly.

Nancy looked at him in surprise. Tyler Scott had said all the neighbors had been questioned.

"Right. Cindy Austin. The twelve-year-old girl who's missing from the Connelly home? The house at the end of this road?" Nancy waved in the general direction of the road.

"I don't know anything about it," Mr. Carver said. "I left late last night for an overnight trip and I just got back."

Nancy's pulse quickened. Here was someone Tyler Scott hadn't questioned! "Cindy was discovered missing around eight o'clock last night," she said. "Were you still home?"

"Sure, I was home at eight. In fact I was packing the car." He looked thoughtful. "I did see a child on a bike about that time. I remember thinking it was kind of late."

"What did she look like?" Nancy asked excitedly. "Do you remember what she was wearing?"

"Well, I don't know. She had a jacket on. It was black, or dark blue, I think."

"Cindy's coat is dark blue!" Nancy was elated. "Which direction was she headed in?"

Mr. Carver spread his palms. "When I saw her, she was just standing still, like she didn't know which way to go. I hollered a hello at her but she bent her head and started off that way." He pointed in the direction toward the highway. "But I don't know if she kept on going or turned off somewhere."

"Thank you, Mr. Carver," Nancy said warmly. "You've been a great help. Would you mind if we have a look around?"

"Sure thing. But don't touch the electric fence out back." He jerked his thumb over his shoulder. "I've got a few head of cattle that pasture on the west side of the barn and I keep them in with the fence. The electricity doesn't hurt them, but it can deliver a mighty jolt to a person."

"What about the cows themselves?" Bess asked nervously.

"Oh, don't mind them." Mr. Carver smiled. "They're as gentle as can be."

Nancy thanked him again. Then she, Bess, and George circled the farmhouse and started checking the outbuildings nearest the house. "Look for any sign of Cindy," Nancy called as Bess and George headed one way and she walked toward the pasture where the cows stood quietly, swishing their tails.

Mr. Carver's words worried Nancy. She now believed Cindy must have traveled farther than she'd first thought. Could she have made it all the way to River Heights?

Nancy carefully ducked under the two strands of electric fencing. She could hear the hum of the voltage.

The red-and-white Herefords eyed Nancy with disinterest as she rapidly crossed the field and headed for a stand of oaks. When she reached the towering trees she felt a keen sense of disappointment. Though the oaks provided some shelter, they weren't dense enough to protect anyone. Most of their leaves had fallen and the ground

24

beneath them was soggy and damp. Cindy was much more likely to hide in one of the buildings on the farm.

Nancy shivered and glanced around. It almost felt as if someone were watching her. She gazed across the damp fields, but saw nothing suspicious.

It must be my imagination, she thought.

Retracing her steps, Nancy arrived at the bright red cattle barn. She searched the ground floor first, examining several empty stalls. But all she found were farming tools and supplies and a pair of black rubber boots spattered with mud. The boots had to belong to Mr. Carver; they were much too large for Cindy.

Climbing to the hayloft, Nancy waved out the open window to Bess and George. George signaled that she and Bess had checked the outbuildings and were going to cross the road and hunt on the other side of Mr. Carver's property.

Nancy climbed down the ladder, dusting her hands on her jeans. The place was dry and quiet. It would be a perfect hideout for Cindy, yet there was no sign of her. Nancy sighed. She suspected that, even though he hadn't spoken to Mr. Carver, Tyler Scott had probably already searched Carver's property. Cindy simply wasn't there.

After walking back through the tall grass, Nancy searched the shed where the power for the electric fence was located. It, too, was empty.

She stepped back outside, her gaze sweeping

the whole area. The cows chewed their cuds and looked bored. Nancy walked along the edge of the fence. Nothing. There was nowhere Cindy could be.

Retracing her footsteps, Nancy ducked her head beneath the electric fence near the shed. Behind her, she heard a scrunching noise. Turning, she started to lift her head. Strong hands suddenly pushed her to her knees. She caught sight of a pair of black rubber boots and dark slacks.

"Hey—!"

Before she could say anything else, the hands picked her up and thrust her against the humming wires! A jolt of fire shot through her, and she crumpled limply to the ground.

4

Detour

Dimly, Nancy became aware of voices. She heard Bess. And George. They were arguing loudly nearby. She tried to lift her eyelids but they felt weighted down.

". . . someone did that to her deliberately," George was saying angrily. "Why don't you try to find out who that someone is!"

"Miss Fayne," came Tyler Scott's cold voice, "if Miss Drew was truly pushed into that electric wire, it's all the more reason why she should give up trying to find Cindy Austin. It's too dangerous."

Nancy's eyes shot open. She was lying on some kind of table in what looked like a hospital emergency room. George was glaring furiously at the head of the Austins' security team, and Bess was standing nearby, her face white.

27

Seeing Nancy open her eyes, Bess cried, "Nancy! You're awake!"

Everyone rushed over to her, but when Nancy sat up and tried to climb off the hospital table, one of the nurses gently, but firmly, pushed her down. "Wait a few moments, Miss Drew. You tangled with a lot of voltage, and you need to rest."

"I'm fine," Nancy managed to say. It was true. She was feeling better by the second.

"Wait until the doctor examines you," the nurse said on her way out of the room. "He'll be right in."

"Are we at the hospital?" Nancy asked, looking around.

"That's right," Tyler Scott cut in before Bess or George could speak. "Your friends seem to feel you were pushed into that electric wire."

"She was!" George said hotly. "The voltage was cranked up to its maximum. Mr. Carver didn't do that, and we certainly didn't. Someone tampered with the voltage box, then pushed Nancy into the fence!"

"I *was* pushed," Nancy said. "I remember seeing—" She cut herself off and instead glanced down at Tyler Scott's feet. He wore brown shoes, but his slacks were of some dark material. Could he have pulled the black boots over his shoes and afterward taken them off?

"We tried to call your dad but he wasn't in his office," said Bess.

28

"No problem, I'll tell him about this when I get home." Nancy was glad her father hadn't been alarmed.

"Mr. Carver's right outside the room," George remarked. "He said that, even at full voltage, there isn't enough power in the fence to kill someone, but the person who pushed you probably didn't know that. Nancy, somebody meant to kill you!"

Tyler Scott's mouth was knife-blade thin. "That's a lot of suppositions, Miss Fayne." He turned to Nancy. "Luckily, I ordered one of my men to follow you today. Wiggins found you and brought you and your friends to the hospital."

The doctor arrived and everyone but Nancy was asked to leave the room. After a brief examination the doctor pronounced Nancy well enough to check out. As Nancy walked out of the room, she saw Mr. Carver and Tyler's man, John Wiggins, waiting anxiously outside. They both wore dark pants but neither man had on black boots.

Mr. Carver was tremendously relieved to see Nancy on her feet. "I don't know what could have happened. I checked that voltage before I left last night. It wasn't near that high."

"Someone must have raised it," Nancy murmured, thinking hard. Why had she been pushed into the fence? Clearly, someone didn't want her to find Cindy. But who? And why? It didn't make sense, unless Cindy had been truly kidnapped and the kidnappers didn't want Nancy getting too close to the truth!

Wiggins made a sound of exasperation. He had a heavy, glum face and seemed as annoyed with her as Tyler Scott was. "You're lucky you weren't killed," he said angrily. "What did you think you were doing? Don't you know anything about electricity?"

Nancy's blue eyes flashed. "I was pushed, Mr. Wiggins. And I certainly didn't raise the voltage on the fence! It's apparent someone doesn't want me searching for Cindy Austin."

Reassuring George and Bess that she was fine, Nancy dropped her two friends off and headed back to the Connellys'. As soon as she stepped through the door, Barbara Austin clasped Nancy's hands in her own. "Thank goodness you're all right! When Tyler called and told me what happened I was so frightened."

Tyler Scott has certainly done a great job of alarming the Austins, Nancy thought to herself. Would she be able to undo the damage?

Barbara cleared her throat and glanced at her husband. "Terence and I have been talking, Nancy, and we both think it would be better if you were off this case."

Nancy was glad Tyler Scott wasn't there. She could just imagine his satisfied expression.

"I've been in tight spots before," Nancy assured Barbara. "And I've always managed to take care of myself. Besides, after this incident, I think the more people searching for Cindy the better."

At that moment Katherine entered the room. "I couldn't help overhearing what you were saying," she said. "I think taking Nancy off the case is a big mistake. She's good at what she does."

Barbara looked torn. "Maybe we should call in the police. They'll find Cindy and this whole thing will be over."

"Barbara—" Nancy broke in, but before she could go on Terence Austin interrupted.

"Bringing the police into this affair now will only cause a lot of publicity," he said firmly. "Reporters will start asking questions. Within days the results of our research will be all over the front pages. And if that happens . . ." He abruptly ended the thought and paced across the room. "Cindy's done this kind of thing before. We all know it. All we need is a few more hours. If news of our research—and our whereabouts—should leak out, Cindy's life could be in even more danger."

Barbara and Terence exchanged agonized looks. However, Terence's next words took Nancy by complete surprise. "We'll keep you on the case, Nancy." He took a deep breath. "Now, tell us the truth. What do you really think has happened to our daughter?"

All heads turned toward Nancy. She hesitated,

then said softly, "I believe Cindy left on her own." Nancy told them about Mr. Carver seeing a cyclist, and Tyler Scott's theory that Cindy left because she wanted to prove she was a better detective than Nancy.

"Do you really think that's the reason?" Katherine asked.

"I don't know. But she wouldn't just take off without some reason. She's only been to a few places in River Heights, and she's unfamiliar with the town." Nancy grew thoughtful. "In fact, what places have you been to since you arrived?"

"Cindy and I went to the mall once," Barbara said. "The one on the east side of town. And we went to the museum and the park."

"We've been to two restaurants, too," Terence put in, listing their names for Nancy. "But what does this have to do with anything?"

Nancy shrugged. "We know that Cindy left on her own. I'm hoping she headed for someplace she was familiar with. It'll at least give me a place to start." She smiled reassuringly. "Anywhere else?"

"Your father's office," Barbara said after some thought. "We met Katherine for lunch there. That's the same day we went to the mall."

Privately, Nancy felt there was no way Cindy would be at either the mall, or her father's office. The mall was in the opposite direction from Mr. Carver's farmhouse. Her father's office was heavily secured and offered no place to hide.

Pulling on her jacket, Nancy said, "I'll ask Dad if he's seen anything."

Barbara Austin again clasped Nancy's hands in her own. "Thanks, Nancy. I'm sure you wondered what to think, the way I insisted Cindy had been kidnapped. I'm relieved to learn you truly believe she left on her own. But I'm furious with her for putting us through this!"

Barbara doesn't really sound furious, Nancy thought with an inward smile. She sounds anxious and hopeful.

"I'll let you know if I find out anything," Nancy promised.

Fifteen minutes later Nancy was on her way home. Rain had begun falling steadily and the night was dark. As she drove, Nancy tried to think where Cindy might be hiding. Although she was convinced Cindy had left on her own, she was also convinced that Cindy was in danger. Whoever had pushed Nancy into that fence had been desperate. But why?

If it's a game of wits, Nancy thought, then Cindy's left me some clue. Had the misspelled rhyme been left for her? "Moffett," Nancy said aloud, wondering why it seemed familiar.

The wipers slapped rain from the windshield as Nancy considered. Moffett. Why did the word *Moffett* make her think of farmland? Was that because she'd been at Mr. Carver's farm today? "Moffett . . ." she said again.

She hit a large pool of water and skidded

sideways for a few seconds before her wheels caught the pavement again. Where could Cindy be hiding on a night like tonight? She must have some kind of shelter.

An orange sign with black arrows marked Detour loomed in front of her, and Nancy automatically turned off the road onto a rutted dirt track. As her wheels bumped over rocks and slid in muddy pools, she thought, I don't remember a Detour sign on the way in.

Nancy drove ahead cautiously, straining to see through the inky night. Had the rain caused some damage to the main road? This detour seemed little better than a trail.

Empty blackness suddenly appeared before her. There were no more trees and bushes. Nancy jammed on the brakes. Her headlights dipped forward, bobbing crazily into a black hole.

She was perched on the edge of a deep ravine!

"Oh, no!" she gasped, seeing the bottom of the cliff far below. But it was too late. Her wheels slid forward.

She was falling over the edge!

5

Death Squeeze

Shifting into reverse gear, Nancy closed her eyes and braced for the crash. Her car teetered on the edge of the cliff. She counted her heartbeats. The car stayed poised on the edge.

Reaching blindly for the door handle, Nancy scrambled out, slipping and sliding through the mud to safety.

Soft rain fell on her head as she glanced back. Her blue sports car hung on the edge, its engine still humming. But it wasn't going over!

"Unreal," Nancy muttered, heaving a sigh of relief as her pounding heart slowed. Why had the Detour sign been placed on the road? Why weren't there any blockades to prevent a car from being driven over this cliff?

Across the ravine Nancy could see twin ruts where the road took up again.

Moving carefully, she returned to her car. The front wheels were over the edge but the main body was stuck against the ground. Nancy thought about climbing inside and turning off the engine but changed her mind. It was too dangerous. The only thing to do was find help.

Trudging back down the muddy road, she noticed something glowing in the bushes. She drew back the wet leaves and saw a white sign which read Caution: Bridge Out. Someone had deliberately knocked down the sign and hidden it, she realized grimly.

Nancy hauled up the sign and carried it to where the dirt track forked off the main highway. She then removed the Detour sign and propped the Caution sign up in its place. Now cars would keep to the highway and no one would be hurt.

Who had this trap been meant for? she wondered. *Her?*

"Well, it proves one thing," she said under her breath as she walked back toward the Connellys'. "Even though Cindy left on her own, someone doesn't want me to find her. And that someone has to be watching the house!"

"Nancy!" Katherine Connelly's eyes widened when she saw the mud-covered detective.

"I had a little trouble with my car," Nancy explained with a smile, knowing what she must look like. "Mind if I use your phone?"

36

"What happened?" Barbara Austin demanded fearfully as Nancy wiped her feet on the mat.

Nancy hesitated. She wasn't certain she wanted to reveal the truth about her accident. Tyler Scott had already nearly convinced the Austins to take her off the case. But she had to make some kind of explanation. "I took a wrong turn where the highway straightens on that last stretch toward River Heights."

"A wrong turn?" Katherine was puzzled. "But, Nancy, there are just dirt roads on either side of the highway."

Barbara said to Nancy, "Something happened, didn't it?"

When Nancy didn't answer right away, Terence said, watching her closely, "There have been entirely too many accidents for one day, Nancy. Suppose you tell us the *whole* truth."

"I will. But please keep in mind that taking me off the case now might not be the best solution."

Terence's concerned expression softened and Nancy saw the trace of a smile on his lips. "All right. I've been warned. What happened?"

Nancy related what had taken place on the dirt road. Barbara paled and Terence looked alarmed. Only Katherine listened objectively.

"So what's your theory, Nancy?" she asked.

Nancy took a deep breath. "I think someone deliberately tried to kill me. Or at least get me out of the way for a little while," she added quickly.

A shadow fell across the living room carpet and Nancy glanced up to see Tyler Scott standing in the doorway. "You're certain it was deliberate, Miss Drew?" he demanded. Like Nancy, he was soaking wet and she realized he must have been out searching for Cindy.

A terrible thought occurred to her. Could *Tyler* have been the one who changed the signs? Whoever rigged the trap must have known she was at the Connellys'. That meant someone in the household was involved, or at the very least, was leaking information.

"That Detour sign was put up to make sure I took that dirt road, and the Bridge Out sign had been hidden in the bushes. It was deliberate," Nancy replied. Casually, she glanced down at Tyler Scott's shoes, but although they were wet, they had no mud on them.

"Nancy, do you really believe someone is after you?" Katherine asked, frowning.

"That Detour sign had to have been put up recently. Otherwise another car would have taken the detour and ended up at the ravine before I did. I think whoever changed the signs knew I would be the only one leaving here tonight."

"But how would anyone know that?" Barbara asked, swallowing. "No one knows our hourly plans!"

"Except the people in this household," Tyler Scott said, his gaze hardening. "Just what are you suggesting, Miss Drew?"

Nancy couldn't help wondering about Tyler, Wiggins, and Katz. They were the most likely candidates. Tyler was actually staying at the Connellys', and Wiggins and Katz spent most of their time there, too. Promising herself she would investigate them all more thoroughly, Nancy said to Barbara and Terence, "I think your enemies are watching you very closely. They probably know Cindy has run away. We need to redouble our efforts to find her before she gets into real trouble."

"Thank you for sharing your wisdom and experience, Miss Drew," Tyler said mockingly. "I'm sure we've all learned something we didn't know."

Nancy flushed, and Terence shot a dark look at the security man. "I think that'll do it for tonight, Tyler," he said.

"Fine." Tyler turned on his heel.

After Tyler left, Terence turned to Nancy. "I know you're eager to stay on the case, Nancy, but it's growing more and more dangerous. As much as I want my little girl back, I can't risk your life."

Nancy didn't say anything. Was he about to take her off the case?

"Let us think about it overnight. If Cindy hasn't been found by tomorrow morning or come back on her own, some decisions are going to have to be made."

"I understand."

Seeing she could plead with Terence and Barbara no further, Nancy left the room to call for a tow truck. Barbara Austin's voice followed Nancy through the open doorway to the living room. "Terence, I'm scared," she said, her voice trembling. "You don't think the Master has her, do you?"

"Shhh." Terence's voice lowered but Nancy could still hear. "Cindy's out there on her own. Let's just hope Nancy or Tyler finds her before the Master finds out she's missing."

The door closed and Nancy heard no more. The Master? Nancy thought to herself. Who's the Master?

As Nancy hung up the phone, still pondering the conversation she'd just overheard, she turned to find Katherine at her elbow.

"Do you need a ride home?" Katherine asked.

"I'm temporarily without wheels," Nancy admitted, "but I think I'll call my friend George and see if she can come and get me. Thanks, anyway."

Nancy called and found George and Bess together. Hearing Nancy's plight, they quickly drove to the Connellys' and picked her up.

"But who would do such a thing?" Bess asked as soon as they were on their way home. "Why wouldn't they want you to find Cindy?"

"I don't really know," Nancy admitted. "The Austins are working on a secret government project and they've told me they have enemies who would like to get their hands on their research.

Maybe one of their enemies hopes to find Cindy first."

"And ask for a ransom?" George's brows lifted.

"No one's said that, but I think it's on everyone's mind." Nancy glanced down at her mud-smeared jeans and jacket. "I'm just lucky the accident wasn't any worse." She frowned. "Somehow information's leaking out about what's going on at the Connellys'. That Detour sign was moved on purpose; somebody knew I was leaving. Either the place is being watched, or someone on the inside is a traitor."

"Who?" Bess and George echoed together.

"I'd like to think it's Tyler Scott," Nancy said. "That man rubs me the wrong way. But I don't have any evidence."

George pulled up at Nancy's house, and Bess and George accepted her invitation to come in for a cup of cocoa, some popcorn, and a late movie on television. Nancy quickly changed her clothes then joined her friends in front of the TV. Bess and George were already in the middle of an argument.

"I don't care what you say." Bess tossed her pretty, blond head. "We're going to beat Chatham Central Friday night!"

Nancy smiled. "I didn't know you paid so much attention to football, Bess."

"I don't." She shot George a glance of annoyance. "I just get it drilled into my head all the

time, so I figured I'd argue the way *she* does."
She jerked a thumb in George's direction.

Ignoring Bess, George said to Nancy, "Let's get back to Cindy. Where do you think she could be?"

"Barbara Austin told me some of the places she's visited since she's been in River Heights and I've been trying to decide if they have anything to do with the nursery rhyme Cindy left." Nancy brought Cindy's notebook downstairs and showed Bess and George the misspelled rhyme.

"Moffett," George said, making a face.

"Does it sound familiar to you?" Nancy asked. "It rings a bell with me but I can't place it. I keep thinking it has something to do with land."

"Isn't there a street called Moffett?" Bess ventured timidly. "Somewhere . . . ?"

"Of course!" Nancy leaped to her feet. "Moffett Way! It's out by——" She suddenly snapped her fingers, her eyes sparkling. "I've got it! About five years ago a man named Moffett donated all that land on the east side of town to the city. In fact originally they were going to name Riverfront Park *Moffett* Park!"

George rose from the couch, too, her dark eyes alight with excitement. "So you think . . ."

"That Cindy's hiding out at the park. Barbara even said they'd visited the park!"

"Let's go!" George shouted, and she and Nancy bolted for the door.

42

"To the park?" Bess asked. "But it's dark. And it's so late. The park might be closed." Bess got a disgusted glance from her cousin. "Well, I guess if you really think Cindy's there . . ."

"Come on," Nancy urged. "We've got to get out there."

As they hurried to George's car Nancy saw someone duck behind a hedge across the street. Something about the bulky figure seemed familiar. She glanced back twice as George pulled out of the driveway. But apart from the softly falling rain shimmering in the light from the streetlamp, she saw nothing. Perhaps she had imagined the shadow.

George headed directly toward Riverfront Park, but Nancy said, "Drive around for a while first. I want to make sure no one's following us."

George did as Nancy suggested, driving into the heart of River Heights and winding in and out of some of the city's narrowest streets. Nancy kept glancing back. The road behind them was empty.

"That enough?" George asked as they wound around another tight corner.

"So far, so good," Nancy murmured.

As they turned onto Moffett Way, Nancy glimpsed the ivy-covered walls of Chatham Central High School. There were several dark cars parked at the curb but none followed after them as they swept by.

By the time George's car was passing beneath

the arched hedge that crowned the park's entry, even Nancy was convinced no one could have followed them. "Now all we have to worry about is Cindy," Nancy said. "Let's cut the lights and sneak in."

"Your wish is my command," George said, and she clicked off the headlights of the station wagon.

The car moved forward like a shadow. The towering trees made the park seem dark and eerie. Bess scrunched down in her seat. "Let me know when it's over," she said.

George drove quietly toward the center of the park. A small octagonal building, a gazebo, stood in the middle of a grassy circle. Pulling the car to the side of the road, George cut the engine. She and Nancy climbed out. The rain had stopped but the ground was wet and soggy.

From the backseat Bess whispered, "I think I'll wait here and keep a lookout."

"Good idea," Nancy agreed, then she and George crossed the footpath that led to the gazebo's steps.

Wind rattled raindrops from the leaves in the trees and caused both girls to shiver. Standing in the center of the gazebo they looked in all directions.

"There's nowhere here that Cindy could hide," Nancy said, disappointed. "And this is the only structure in the park."

"She couldn't even crawl beneath it," George

observed. "The floorboards are too close to the ground." She glanced at Nancy. "Now what?"

"I don't think she's here," Nancy murmured. "I was so sure that clue meant the park. Maybe it's—"

Nancy's voice died in her throat. Through the trees headlights flickered. George followed her gaze. They both waited and watched. Soon a car rounded the last bend. When its headlights swept the back of George's car, its own lights were switched off!

"Quick! Hide!" Nancy ordered, and dove into a thicket of bushes. George tumbled down beside her.

"Who is it?" George asked tensely.

"I don't know. But they're acting strangely. If they get out of their car we're going to have to do something." Nancy was grave. "I'm worried about Bess. Come on, let's move closer."

George followed Nancy through the bushes. Wet leaves brushed their faces. The other car, a black sedan, slowed to a stop behind George's, its engine still thrumming. Squinting, Nancy could make out two dim figures in the front seat. She glanced at George's car. There was no sign of Bess!

"I wish they'd get out of the car so I could see them," Nancy muttered.

"I'll bet Bess is paralyzed with fright!" George replied.

The black sedan's headlights flashed back on.

45

Its engine revved. With a screech of tires, the car suddenly wheeled around George's station wagon and tore off through the park.

Nancy and George ran. George jumped behind the wheel of her car and Nancy slid into the passenger seat. "Bess?" Nancy called anxiously, peering at the backseat.

Bess's blond head popped up. Her eyes were huge and scared. "What's going on?" she asked as she uncurled her body and sat up.

"We're the ones doing the following now," George muttered with relish, slamming the station wagon into gear. "Two can play this game!"

The car jumped forward. Driving as fast as she dared, George quickly caught up to the other car. Its taillights glowed red as it turned on the road ahead of her.

"I wish I could read the license number. Can you catch up to them?" Nancy asked anxiously.

"Just watch me. . . ."

Tires squealed as George turned a corner. Nancy braced herself for a crash, but George yanked the wheel around.

"You're gaining," Bess breathed.

"Come on, come on . . ." George muttered.

Suddenly everything happened at once. The black sedan veered off the road. Before George could do the same, blinding lights flashed in her rearview mirror. Nancy glanced back. Another car! And this one was gaining fast!

George charged after the first car. *Bang!* The

car behind suddenly slammed into them. Bess screamed and Nancy was jolted forward until her seat belt caught.

"What the . . . ?" George asked, craning her neck.

Bang! Bang! Nancy clung to the dash. "They're ramming into us!" she yelled breathlessly. "They're trying to drive us off the road!"

Bang! Bang! Bang! Slamming her foot on the accelerator, George practically pulled the station wagon forward. The car skidded sideways through a patch of mud. Then the wheels touched pavement and she cranked the car to the right. Suddenly the sedan she'd been pursuing was right in front of her!

"There's—" Nancy said, then the car behind slammed into George's, locking bumpers. Stepping on the accelerator again, George tried to surge forward. Nancy glanced at the car in front of them. Its back-up lights suddenly switched on.

Nancy watched in disbelief as the car in front reversed straight at them. They were going to be crushed between the two cars!

6

Shadowy Figure

George spun the steering wheel. With a scream of wrenching metal her bumper unhooked from the car that had rammed them. Careening sideways, the station wagon whipped mud from its back tires, splattering the car behind. George stomped on the accelerator, tore across the bumpy ground, and raced past the car reversing toward them. Nancy and Bess hung on, not daring to breathe.

Nancy glanced in the rearview mirror. "They're both chasing us," she said through clenched teeth.

"They haven't seen anything yet," George said determinedly. She held the steering wheel steady as she accelerated. The station wagon surged forward toward the park's entrance.

Nancy's mind was ticking off the possibilities. There was nothing to do but run for it. "Get us out of here, George," she said. "And then go like lightning!"

Headlights were closing in on them as they reached the main gate. Nancy glanced both ways. "The road's clear," she yelled. The station wagon tore onto the open road.

"They're dropping behind!" Bess cried in relief.

"They're letting us get away," Nancy said, seeing the other cars' headlights disappear as George swept over a rise. "I wish I could have gotten their license numbers—but don't stop! Whatever you do, don't stop."

"Hurry, George!" Bess urged.

George made a noise that sounded suspiciously like a chuckle. "Don't worry," she said. "We're home free." With a burst of speed they left Riverfront Park and their pursuers far behind.

The next morning, as Nancy went into the kitchen, Carson Drew was just rising from the table, folding his newspaper. "Katherine phoned. Cindy's still missing. Katherine's meeting me at work this morning," he told Nancy as she seated herself at the table. "She has to get a few things done at the office and she asked me if you would mind stopping by to see Barbara this morning."

"I'd love to, but I don't have a car." She sighed. "Terence said he'd call and let me know if he still wants me on the case."

Hannah, the Drews' housekeeper, set a plate of bacon and eggs in front of Nancy and said, "Maybe some good food will wipe that scowl off your face."

"Am I scowling?" Nancy was surprised.

"It looks more like severe concentration to me," Carson Drew replied with a smile. "If you're having trouble with your car, you can drop me off at work and take my car, if you'd like."

"Thanks, but I'd hate to wreck another one."

"What do you mean?"

Nancy briefly recounted the events of the night before, ending with, "I'd better call George and make certain everything's all right. The damage didn't look too bad, but you never know."

"Did you get a look at the people in the cars?" Carson Drew asked soberly.

Nancy shook her head. "*How* did they find us?"

"You think they were after Cindy?"

Nancy nodded. "And I think it's all connected with the Austins' research. Cindy left on her own, but I'd bet whoever chased us would like to get their hands on her. Then they could demand a ransom for her release."

"Unfortunately, I think you're right," said Carson Drew. He picked up his briefcase. "Be careful, Nancy. You're sure you don't want my car?"

Nancy regarded her father affectionately. Though he'd been alarmed by her two narrow escapes the day before, he still trusted her.

"Okay, I'll take you to work then drive to the Connellys' and back," she promised. "My car should be ready then. Thanks."

"I'll ask Katherine for a lift home," he said, and they walked out the door together.

Nancy dropped her father at his office. Before going to the Connellys' she stopped at George's house and picked her up.

"How's the car?" Nancy asked uncomfortably when they were on their way.

"Not bad," George assured her. "The bumper's twisted and one of the taillights is broken but otherwise it's okay. My parents are just glad we weren't hurt."

"So am I," Nancy said feelingly. "Whoever was after us meant business."

"Who do you think they were?"

"I don't know. But I mean to find out."

Barbara and Terence were seated at the dining room table drinking coffee when George and Nancy arrived. On seeing Nancy, Barbara got to her feet and came over and hugged her. "Lieutenant Bennington is coming by. Terence called the police this morning, and since Cindy's been missing for over twenty-four hours, they're going to start searching for her."

Nancy wondered how Tyler Scott felt about that. She was about to ask when she glanced through the window and saw the man himself pull into the driveway. He and John Wiggins and Ray Katz climbed out of a black sedan at the same

51

time. Nancy's breath caught. She'd forgotten Tyler Scott drove a black sedan. It looked just like the car that had rammed them!

She scanned the front of the vehicle, but there was no sign of mud or damage. It hadn't been Tyler's car in Riverfront Park the night before.

"Uh-oh, here comes trouble," George said into Nancy's ear as Tyler walked into the house.

Terence cleared his throat and said, "Tyler, I'd like to talk to you for a minute."

Signaling the other men to go on ahead of him, Tyler strode into the dining room. He looked tired and serious. Nancy wondered if he'd been out searching for Cindy all night.

"I just wanted you to know we've called the police," Dr. Austin said quietly.

"*What?*" Tyler's jaw dropped.

"Our daughter's out there somewhere. I think we need help finding her before someone really kidnaps her."

"Do you know what kind of a security risk this is?" Tyler hissed.

"Yes. But our daughter's more important."

This was clearly not how Tyler Scott felt. He glared at Nancy as if it were all her fault, and seeing his look, Barbara put in, "If Nancy wants to stay on the case she's more than welcome. We need all the help we can get."

Tyler started to argue but at that moment Lieutenant Bennington's car pulled up behind Tyler's. Tyler clamped his jaw shut and waited for the police officer to be admitted. Once they were all in the room Tyler introduced everyone and then stated flatly, "My job is to maintain security here. Cindy must be found, but frankly, even if she is it's no guarantee that she won't take off again. She's done this kind of thing more than once."

"Is that correct, Dr. Austin?" Lieutenant Bennington opened his notebook and looked at Terence Austin.

"Yes." Terence's lips were tight.

"Where do you think she would be most likely to go?"

"We've looked in all the likely places," Tyler put in. "We've even employed the talents of Nancy Drew here."

His tone suggested he thought Nancy's involvement was a joke, and Lieutenant Bennington narrowed his gaze at her.

Nancy was acquainted only slightly with the young lieutenant. He hadn't been with the force very long, but she had the uncomfortable feeling he would be more interested in making a name for himself by cracking some other big case than in finding a young runaway.

Lieutenant Bennington asked more questions and jotted down some notes. He requested a recent photograph of Cindy, and Barbara found one and gave it to him.

Snapping shut his notebook, Bennington said, "I'll see what I can do," then headed out the door. His entire visit had lasted less than five minutes.

There was a smugness around Tyler's mouth. Nancy frowned. She suspected he was pleased that he'd made Cindy's disappearance sound like a common occurrence. And Bennington's lack of interest didn't help matters.

Nancy sensed that Terence and Barbara Austin weren't happy, however. After Tyler left the room Terence glanced wryly at Nancy. "I'm sorry, Nancy. I know I have no right to ask after what I said last night, but I hope you haven't given up."

"No, I haven't. George and I will search some more this afternoon."

"Thank you, Nancy," Barbara said with gratitude.

The rain had begun again as Nancy and George scoured the area in a widening circle from the Connelly home. They drove to the park again and hunted for any signs of Cindy. Finally they stopped searching, picked up Nancy's car, and then met at the Drew home.

"I feel like I'm going around and around in circles," Nancy complained as she shook rain from her hair and flopped down on one of the kitchen chairs. "I need to think."

"Let's call Bess and have a brainstorming session," George suggested. "There's been so much happening, we haven't had time to go over the

54

case. We can go to Tony's, eat huge amounts of food, and think."

Nancy couldn't argue with such appetizing logic. "Good idea. I'll bring Cindy's notebook with me."

They picked up Bess and headed for Tony's Italian Restaurant. Nancy drove in the direction of Riverfront Park, turning off Moffett Way onto Kingsman Road and traveling past Chatham Central High School. A banner stretched across the brick archway of the school read: Come Watch the Wildcats Pounce on River Heights on Friday Night!

"I think they're being overly optimistic." George sniffed.

"Is Ned coming to the game?" asked Bess.

"I hope so," Nancy said. "He's supposed to call sometime this week and let me know."

Nancy parked on the street in front of the restaurant. Tony's was little more than a café, but it was popular for its tasty yet inexpensive pasta dishes. When Nancy, Bess, and George walked inside, the restaurant was already crowded with students from Chatham Central.

"Hi, Nancy!" Nancy's friend Christine O'Callaghan emerged from the group, wearing her green-and-gold Chatham Central cheerleading uniform. "You River Heights grads are sure brave to meet us on our territory!"

"They won't be here after Friday night," yelled

a young man standing behind her. "They'll be too ashamed."

"You laugh now," George said, grinning, "but those who laugh last, laugh best."

"Ha, ha, ha!" was the response.

There were more catcalls and teasing remarks as Nancy and her friends ordered their food, and for a while Nancy got caught up in the friendly rivalry between the two schools.

"There's Coach Phillips!" someone yelled and Nancy turned to look at the smiling man who'd just entered the restaurant.

He raised his hand in a fist of victory. "Friday," was all he said, and the crowd of students chanted, "Wildcats! Wildcats! Wildcats!" until George rolled her eyes and clapped her hands over her ears.

"Whose idea was it to come here?" she complained.

"Yours!" Nancy and Bess reminded her together.

By the time their manicotti, deep dish pizza, and spaghetti arrived, the place had calmed down. Seated at a window table, Nancy stared out at the rain, her thoughts turning once again to Cindy. "I'm really worried about Cindy," she admitted. "Those people last night were serious."

George dug into her spaghetti, twirling it onto her fork. "What have we got so far?"

"Someone pushed me into the electric fence,"

Nancy said reflectively. "That someone may or may not have meant to kill me, but whoever it was wanted me out of the way."

"The only person I know who wants you off the case is Tyler Scott," said Bess.

"And he drives a black sedan," George pointed out. "We saw it today. You said yourself someone inside the house has to be leaking information. It has to be Scott."

"But the front of his car wasn't smashed at all," Nancy said, shaking her head.

"Maybe he got it fixed already," Bess suggested. "Or maybe it was the front car. That one wasn't damaged."

"Both cars were black sedans. There were at least three people involved last night," Nancy mused. "Two in the front car and at least one in the back."

"Tyler Scott and his two men," Bess declared, biting into a thick slice of double-cheese pizza.

"It's too much of a coincidence that Tyler Scott drives a black sedan and both cars last night were of the same color and type." Nancy bit thoughtfully on her lower lip. "Unfortunately, it doesn't help us find Cindy. Whoever chased us is looking for her, too."

Bess and George both nodded. Glancing out the window, Bess asked, "Who's that?"

Nancy followed her gaze. Outside, a dark, shadowy figure stood beneath the dripping eave of a building on the other side of the street. "The bus comes by here. Maybe he's waiting for a ride."

"Well, he's acting strange. He was on the curb but he ducked back out of sight when he saw me looking his way."

"Sounds to me like you're getting paranoid," George remarked, and Bess made a face at her.

Nancy watched the stranger out of the corner of her eye as she picked up another forkful of manicotti. "He does seem determined to stay out of sight."

Bess gave George a look that said, "See?" but George was still watching the man in question.

"He's left," she said. "He just disappeared around that corner."

Vaguely uneasy, Nancy watched for several minutes but the shadowy stranger didn't return. She purposely pushed him out of her mind and got back to the case. "What did Cindy mean by Little Miss Moffett? Doesn't it have to be Moffett Way? And Barbara said they'd gone to the park. It seems to make sense."

George frowned. "But she wasn't at the park. And besides, she'd be soaking wet if she were."

"So where is she?" Nancy asked. "Where could she be that would be safe and dry and no one would find her? Where would you go?" she asked her two friends.

"I'd go someplace that was near food," Bess said.

George grinned. "This is not news, Bess."

"Well, I would! Wouldn't you? She's got to eat somehow."

"That's right. . . ." Nancy stared off into the distance. "You know, maybe I've been jumping to conclusions. I've just assumed she went somewhere she was familiar with."

"You mean she just *found* a hideout?" George asked. "Isn't that expecting a lot of a twelve-year-old?"

"Maybe it's just someplace she's heard of. She does possess a genius IQ," Nancy reminded both Bess and George. "She's quick-thinking and resourceful and she's got a thing about being a detective. She wants to beat me at my own game." Nancy sighed and pushed her plate to one side. "Moffett Way. I wonder . . ."

A movement outside the window caught Nancy's eye. The man in the shadows had returned, and for an instant she caught a glimpse of his profile. Her heart jumped. He seemed so familiar! Had she seen him somewhere before?

"That man's back," she whispered. "I can't see his face but I'm sure we've met before . . ."

"What are you doing?" Bess asked as Nancy scraped back her chair.

"I'm going to ask him who he is," she said determinedly.

"Not without me!" George was right on her heels.

Nancy raced out Tony's front doors, but the stranger was gone. She heard running footsteps

59

pounding down the sidewalk. "Come on!" she shouted, not waiting to see if George was following her.

She tore down through the rain-drenched streets, glad for her running shoes. Losing sight of the man, Nancy stopped, her heart thumping so loudly she could barely hear the sound of George following behind her. Then faintly she heard the man's heavier tread slapping hard on the pavement ahead and to her left.

She charged after him, zigzagging through several dark alleyways that finally led to a small park. The man was just rounding a six-foot-high hedge and Nancy put on a burst of speed. Realizing she'd outrun George, she considered slowing for a split second.

But there was no time. Nancy sprinted for the hedge. Suddenly she heard growling noises coming from the other side, then a man's muttered yell. Nancy raced around the wet bushes and slid into a grassy field.

Before she could gain her footing two sleek black forms bounded forward, leaping through the air, teeth gleaming white in the pale moonlight.

Doberman pinschers! Nancy realized in terror. She threw up her arms just as they lunged for her throat!

7

"So We Meet Again . . ."

She jerked backward, and the dogs knocked her to the ground. She fought to keep them off. They growled at her, pinning her beneath them. In that split second she glimpsed a man's torn pants leg disappearing over the stone fence on the far side of the field.

Drawing in a breath to scream for help, she realized the dogs weren't attacking. Their growls were low, warning rumbles deep in their chests. One had his teeth locked around the sleeve of her jacket, narrowly missing her arm, but neither attempted to bite her. Clearly, they had been trained not to complete attacks.

Suddenly both Dobermans froze to attention and looked in the direction from which they'd bounded. As if by signal, they tore away from her.

Shaken, Nancy lay on the wet grass, panting.

"Hey, Nancy!" George's voice sounded from somewhere behind her.

"Over here," she said, sitting up. Her heart was thundering. What had caused the dogs to leave?

The sleeve of her jacket was ripped but, Nancy knew, if the Dobermans had wanted to, they could have done much more damage.

"What happened?" George asked, alarmed.

Nancy was about to answer her when two bounding black forms streaked into sight. The Dobermans were coming back!

But this time they were on leashes held by a man wearing a dark raincoat. Warily, Nancy watched the man approach. He wasn't the one she'd been chasing, however. This man was too tall and slim; the one she'd followed had been heavyset.

"Are you all right?" the man asked. "I don't know what came over these two. They have a bad habit of breaking away from their leashes, but they've never attacked anyone before." He helped Nancy to her feet, apologizing to her over and over again.

Now the two dogs seemed more like wriggling puppies than menacing killers. They circled around and around, whining and sniffing. Nancy's fear dissolved. Cautiously, she let them smell her hand.

"Maybe they had a reason to attack," she said thoughtfully. "There was a man up ahead of me and when I rounded the corner he was just scrambling over that stone fence. His pants leg was torn. Do you suppose he could have done something to make your dogs attack him?"

"If the man had kicked at them or thrown something at them, the dogs might have attacked, I suppose," the dogs' owner admitted.

"I'll bet that's what happened," said Nancy. She patted the dogs' sleek heads. "I must have frightened them when I slid around the hedge and so they turned on me instead."

"I'm really sorry," the man began again, but Nancy assured him she was unhurt.

As Nancy and George walked back to Tony's, however, Nancy looked at her ripped sleeve and said ruefully, "Another night like these last two and I won't have anything left to wear!"

"You can borrow from me," George answered, laughing, as they reentered Tony's. "I'm just glad those dogs didn't tear you limb from limb."

"You and me both," Nancy said with feeling, and sat down opposite Bess, who was staring at Nancy's ripped sleeve.

Bess's blue eyes widened when Nancy related the Doberman incident to her. "Oh, Nancy! It's just one thing after another with this case. Maybe you should leave it to the police."

"And Tyler Scott?" Nancy asked, making a face. The idea of giving up and letting the smug security man find Cindy was enough to make Nancy double her efforts.

"Are you kidding?" George demanded. "We can't quit now!"

"But it's dangerous. Every time Nancy makes a move, something awful happens." Bess turned to Nancy. "That man must have been following us."

"I don't know," Nancy said. "Last night we made sure no one followed us, and still they found us. It's as if someone knows where we'll be," Nancy said, frowning. "I just wish I could figure out how they know. Who did we tell where we were going to eat?"

"We told our parents," George said. "And you called Hannah."

"Maybe your phone's bugged!" Bess cried.

"But *no one* knew we were going to the park last night," Nancy argued. "No, it's got to be something else." She pulled Cindy's notebook from her purse. "Maybe there's something in here we overlooked. If Cindy's nursery-rhyme clue didn't refer to Riverfront 'Moffett' Park—" She flipped open the notebook.

"What are these pictures?" George asked.

"Well, this must be a picture of the museum," Nancy said, pointing to a sketch of a building with tall pillars. "Cindy went there, too."

"And this is the Connellys' house," George said.

"There's the arch to the park!" Bess said triumphantly.

Nancy peered closely at the sketch. It was true. Cindy had drawn an arch and there were letters

64

written across it. But they were a meaningless jumble. Nancy frowned. "Behind the arch there's a building with a lot of people in it. That's not like anything in the park."

"What are the people doing?" George craned her neck to see.

"Sitting, I guess. Or standing." Nancy turned the page around.

"Maybe they're having a picnic," Bess said, unwilling to give up her theory.

"Inside a building?" George demanded.

"No, they're—" Nancy drew in a swift breath. "Wait a minute! I know what they're doing. George, Bess, I know where Cindy's hiding!"

Ten minutes later Nancy's car slowed to a stop near Chatham Central High School. All the lights were on in the building and the street was lined with cars.

"The school's having some kind of event," Bess said.

"Good. We can sneak in unnoticed."

"You really think Cindy's here?" George asked.

"Look at the clues. We passed the school on the way to the park last night, remember? That side street is Moffett Way and that picture in the notebook, well . . . There's your arch!"

Nancy pointed to the banner, Come Watch the Wildcats Pounce on River Heights on Friday Night!, draped across the entrance to the school.

"The people in Cindy's sketch are students," Nancy went on. "You can't really tell they're at desks. Cindy's drawing is kind of simple. But I'm sure that's what she means."

"Nancy, you're a genius!" Bess cried.

George chuckled. "Don't let Cindy hear you say that. She'll want to prove she's more of a genius than Nancy is!"

They all laughed as they ran up the steps to the school. Once inside Nancy waited by the front door for a while, watching to see if anyone was following them. But the streets were empty.

"Come on," she said. "Let's go."

The school was having an open house and many of the parents, students, and faculty were inside. Nancy, Bess, and George mingled with the crowd, searching all the while for Cindy.

"I can't wait to meet this kid," George said under her breath. "She's got a bizarre sense of humor. Hiding out in a school, for pete's sake!"

"It's the perfect place to fit in," Nancy said. "I'm surprised we didn't think of it before."

After checking out the upper floor, which was mainly classrooms, and the ground floor, which was more of the same, they quietly moved to the basement.

"Shouldn't we have found her by now?" Bess whispered.

"Shhh," George hissed.

Nancy lifted a finger to her lips, then pointed to the end of the hallway. A thin line of light showed at the bottom of a door. Nancy moved forward and pressed her ear to the panels. She thought she heard someone moving around inside.

It could be the janitor, she supposed, but her heartbeat quickened nevertheless. When the sounds within quieted, she pulled a thin metal tool from her wallet.

"Always prepared, our Nancy," George whispered.

Nancy grinned, and inserted the tool into the lock. While George and Bess held their breath, Nancy cautiously twisted the tool. Apart from several faint *clinks* no other sound was heard.

Carefully she turned the knob, inching open the door. The first thing she saw was a row of tables and a bulletin board covered with notices. She stepped into the room. Her heart sank. There was no one inside.

She was about to say as much to Bess and George when she spied another door tucked in between some lockers. The door was slightly ajar and there were lights on inside the room beyond. Nancy walked quickly forward.

She pushed the door open. On the far wall were several vending machines. A young girl with straight brown hair was punching one of the buttons. With a hollow rattle a pop can slid into the opening and the girl reached to grab it.

"So we meet again," Nancy said softly. "Hello, Cindy."

8

A Dangerous Game

Cindy Austin whipped around, her eyes filled with amazement. "Nancy Drew!" she cried, dumbfounded.

She still wore the same jeans and oversize sweater she'd had on at the Connellys'. She looked a little more tired and a lot more rumpled, but the scowl that darkened her face was just the same as Nancy had remembered.

"You didn't think I would find you, did you?" Nancy said gently. "Well, for a while, I wasn't sure I would, either."

Bess and George slipped into the room and Cindy's gaze moved from Nancy to her two friends. "Who are they?" she demanded. "How did you find me? I didn't even get a chance to call and give you the second clue!"

Nancy introduced George and Bess, and George asked, "What second clue?"

"Humpty Dumpty," Cindy admitted.

Nancy mentally reviewed the nursery rhyme. Her eyes sparkled. "Of course! All the king's horses, and all the *king's men*. Chatham Central's address is *Kingsman* Road!"

"I take it you figured out the Little Miss Moffett clue," Cindy muttered, crestfallen.

Nancy almost smiled. Cindy was really upset that she had been found. "Yes, but I got sidetracked at Riverfront Park. Your mother said you'd visited the park and I thought the nursery rhyme meant the park."

Cindy shook her head. "Where could I hide at the park? No, I remembered the school and the names of the streets."

Nancy sat on the edge of a table and folded her arms. "So you decided to match wits with me, didn't you? You rode Julianne's bike to Chatham Central, sneaked in somehow, and then hid out at the school. Tell me, how did you manage today, when school was in session?"

"That was the easiest part of all," Cindy bragged. "No one paid any attention to me. I just walked into classrooms, said I was a new student whose paperwork was being processed, and they'd be getting a notice soon." She shrugged. "No problem."

Bess stared at Cindy as if she were from another planet. "No one asked you any questions?"

"Not a one. They all believed I was a new student."

"And you bought your food through the vending machines," George said, a note of reluctant admiration creeping into her voice. "Where did you sleep?"

"The health room." Cindy's chest puffed out with pride.

"How'd you get in there? Jimmy the lock?" George asked.

"No, the door wasn't locked," Cindy admitted. "But I did put some tape over the latch in case anyone locked the door today. That way I could still get in. Except now I won't get a chance—"

"Did it ever cross your mind to think about your parents?" Nancy interrupted. "They've been worried sick about you."

For a moment Cindy looked contrite, but then she asked, "Why? I can take care of myself."

Remembering how easily they had been followed the night before, Nancy said, "We'll let your parents explain it to you. Let's get out of here."

On the way back to the Connelly house, Cindy ignored Nancy and her friends' silent disapproval. She chattered on about her adventure at the school, her tone scornful of the students and faculty.

"They're so backward," she said airily. "I can't believe anybody learns anything. They should see the stuff I'm learning. I don't think they would even be able to read it!"

Sensing George was about ready to explode, Nancy said quickly, "Well, I don't know, Cindy. Chatham Central's an excellent school. We all graduated from River Heights, the other high school in town, and we seem to be doing all right."

George smiled humorlessly. "That's right. After all, Nancy figured out where you were, didn't she?"

Cindy glared at her and lapsed into silence, her arms hugging her chest, her chin thrust out aggressively. George shot Nancy a look that said clearly, "This kid's a pain in the neck."

Nancy had to hide a smile.

At the Connelly house Nancy raised her hand to knock on the door, but Cindy pushed past her, opened the door, and breezed inside as if she owned the place. "Anybody home?" she yelled, tossing back her hair with a flip of her hand.

George made an angry move toward her, and Nancy grabbed her friend's arm. "Relax," she whispered.

"But she's so awful." George muttered. "Doesn't she even think about her parents' feelings?"

"She doesn't seem to think about anybody's feelings but her own," Bess observed.

A gasp sounded. Footsteps clattered on the stairs. Barbara Austin ran toward her daughter in a rush, tears forming in the corners of her eyes. "Cindy! You're all right. Oh, you're all right!" She hugged her daughter fiercely. "We were so worried!"

"Cindy," Terence Austin said with deep relief. He followed his wife. "You're safe!"

Soon others swarmed into the room, and Julianne catapulted toward Cindy. "You're back! You're back."

Tyler Scott stood by the door, stunned. John Wiggins and Ray Katz seemed uncomfortable. They turned to Tyler for orders.

Cindy suddenly looked about ready to cry, as if she'd finally realized how much trouble she'd caused. Easing herself out of her mother's arms, she said, "Look, I'm fine. I'm sorry if you were all worried about me, but I can take care of myself."

"Cindy," Terence Austin said sternly. "You can*not* take care of yourself." Turning to Nancy, he asked, "Where did you find her?"

Before Nancy could answer, Cindy burst in, "At Chatham Central. See? I was okay. I was hiding in plain sight." Some of her spunk returned and she added with pride, "It took the girl detective a while to figure that one out."

"Cindy!" Barbara Austin was appalled.

"This isn't a game, Cindy," Tyler Scott snapped out. "Leaving here was foolish and

72

dangerous. You jeopardized everything! What if—"

"I'll handle this, Tyler," Terence interrupted smoothly. "Thank you."

Flushing at the dismissal, Tyler turned on his heel. Wiggins and Katz followed him out of the room, talking quietly. Nancy heard one of them remark about someone's limp, but when she turned to look they were gone.

"Thank you, Nancy," Barbara said, her voice unsteady. "We're so grateful to you."

"I would have come home," Cindy burst out, with tears in her eyes. "I was fine. I was safe! You're all overreacting!" Pushing past her mother she ran up the stairs. A moment later her door slammed.

Terence and Barbara looked embarrassed. "Nancy, I—" Terence began, but Nancy interrupted him.

"Don't worry about it. I'm just glad Cindy's back safe and sound."

Terence nodded. Now that he was over his fear it was clear he was angry with Cindy, too.

Nancy glanced at her friends. "We'd better get going," she said, trying to ease the Austins' embarrassment.

"Nancy, you've done more than your share in helping us. Barbara and I both thank you from the bottom of our hearts." Terence solemnly shook her hand. "But I'm afraid our problems are far from over. I have reason to believe our enemies haven't given up. Cindy could still be in danger."

The way he stressed the word *enemies* frightened Barbara. "Terence, you don't think *he's* involved, do you?"

For an answer, Terence said, "Why don't you check on Cindy? I'll be up in a minute." After Barbara left, he said, "Nancy, could I ask you for another favor?"

"Sure."

"I wonder if you would keep an eye on Cindy? Maybe take her on some outings. She's bored but I'm afraid to take her out myself. I think she'd be safer with you."

"I'll be back tomorrow," Nancy answered, ignoring the jab in the ribs George had given her. "We'll all think of something to keep Cindy busy."

"I've already seen this one," Cindy complained, as Nancy, Bess, and George sat down beside her in the movie theater row the next day.

"You have?" Nancy blinked. "Why didn't you say so before I bought the tickets?"

"You didn't ask."

Nancy counted silently to ten. "Okay. I'm sorry. But since we're already here, we might as well try to enjoy it."

Cindy rolled her eyes toward the ceiling.

74

The film turned out to be fast-paced and entertaining, and Nancy was deeply absorbed in the plot when Cindy yanked on her sleeve. "I'm out of popcorn," she said. "I'll just go get another bucket."

"I'll get it for you," Nancy said, rising from her seat.

"I'm not a baby," Cindy answered angrily. "Besides, this is the best part. I'll be right back. I promise."

She flounced up the aisle before Nancy could react. Nancy waited uneasily for a few moments but she couldn't stand not having Cindy in her sight. Finally, Nancy jumped up from her seat and followed after Cindy.

Nancy pushed through the doors from the theater to the lobby. The place was nearly empty as all of the shows had already begun. Cindy was not at the concession stand.

Nancy looked around quickly, then went into the women's restroom. "Cindy?" she called. No answer.

Growing alarmed, Nancy checked each stall. Cindy wasn't inside any of them. Back in the lobby, there was still no sign of her.

"Excuse me," Nancy said to a woman behind the concession counter. "I've lost the girl that was with me. She's wearing a blue coat and she has straight brown hair. She's twelve years old but she looks older."

"Oh, I saw her. It was really strange. That kid just streaked through the lobby like she was running for her life." The woman pointed toward the main doors. "She went that way."

For half a beat Nancy didn't move. Cindy had run away again!

9

Kidnapped!

Nancy raced to the door. She glanced anxiously in all directions. A misting rain darkened the skies, making it hard to see. Nancy searched the entire parking lot. Cindy was nowhere to be found!

Retracing her footsteps, Nancy went back inside the theater. She was furious at Cindy and furious at herself for trusting her. Yanking open the door to the movie she walked blindly toward her seat, her eyes adjusting to the gloom.

"Bess, George," she whispered loudly. "Come, quick. Cindy's missing!"

"What do you mean?" Bess's voice floated toward Nancy in the darkness. She sounded perplexed. "Cindy's right here."

Nancy blinked. To her amazement Bess was right! Cindy was sitting in her seat, her eyes glued to the screen. She sent Nancy a puzzled look, then returned her attention to the movie.

Nancy eased into the seat beside her, feeling foolish. Was she overreacting? She slid the girl a look out of the corner of her eye. She noticed Cindy had no popcorn. And there were dewy beads of water on her jacket.

Cindy had deliberately set her up!

Steaming, Nancy wondered what she should do. Cindy was playing a very dangerous game that could easily backfire on her.

Throughout the rest of the movie, Nancy wondered how to get through to Cindy. Several times Cindy glanced her way, but Nancy kept her gaze on the screen. She needed to think.

On the way home Nancy decided that she needed to have a talk with the Austins, so she dropped Bess and George off first. The rest of the drive to the Connellys' passed in silence. Cindy squirmed uncomfortably in her seat, but Nancy didn't offer any conversation.

Finally Cindy asked, "What's the matter? You act like you're mad or something."

"Really? I wonder why."

"How should I know?" Turning away from Nancy, Cindy stared out the window at the dark night.

Behind them a pair of headlights showed through the blurring rain. Nancy's heart lurched. Were they being followed?

Keeping an eye on the rearview mirror, Nancy asked casually, "Didn't your parents talk to you about the accidents I had while you were missing?"

"Yeah. So?"

"So, those accidents happened because I was looking for you. It's too dangerous for you to run away again."

"I didn't—"

"Yes, you did, Cindy," Nancy cut her off. "You ran out the front door of the theater. The girl behind the concession stand saw you."

Cindy hunched down in her seat. "I don't know what you're talking about."

"Come on, Cindy. You meant for that girl to see you. Then you sneaked back inside and found your seat again. Just to make me search for you." The headlights grew closer and Nancy's heart started thumping.

They were approaching the last stretch of road toward the Connellys'. Nancy stepped on the accelerator and the headlights fell back. Glancing at Cindy, Nancy asked, "What if someone had been waiting for you outside? Waiting for a chance to grab you?"

"You're all paranoid," Cindy answered. "No one wants to kidnap me."

"Cindy, we're being followed right now. That car's been on my tail since we left the River Heights city limits."

Cindy craned her neck to look around. Concern lined her young face. Nancy drove around the last curve and breathed a sigh of relief when she turned into the Connellys' driveway. To her amazement the other car pulled up behind her. It was a black sedan!

"Tyler Scott," Nancy breathed. She stepped from her car and waited tensely.

The driver's door flew open. Instead of Tyler, Ray Katz climbed from the vehicle. He flung Nancy a dark look. "Tyler's orders," he said by way of explanation. "He doesn't want you out there alone with Cindy."

He could have *warned* me, Nancy thought. Taking a stab in the dark, she asked, "Is that why you were following me the other night?"

"This is my first time, Miss Drew." The security man headed for the front porch.

"So we're being followed by the enemy, huh?" Cindy said sarcastically. "I'm *so* scared." She laughed and skipped ahead of Nancy.

Nancy decided it was time to get a few things straight. She walked into the living room. The Austins were seated on the couch. Katherine Connelly was bending down to refill their coffee cups.

Barbara smiled at Nancy. "How was the movie?"

"We had an—interesting time," Nancy answered carefully. "I wonder, could I talk to all of you about something?"

"It isn't Cindy, is it?" Barbara asked, instantly alarmed.

"Well, partially," Nancy admitted. "But first I think I should explain what happened at the park the other night." Quickly and concisely Nancy told about the black sedans trying to crush her, Bess, and George. "I didn't tell you before because I didn't want to worry you," she finished. "And then when Cindy was found I thought everything might be all right."

"But now you don't," Katherine prompted.

"I'm not sure, but Cindy is still playing her games with me."

"What do you mean?" Terence set down his coffee cup. "What games?"

When Nancy explained what had taken place at the theater, Terence's face darkened with anger. Barbara went white. "She doesn't understand," she murmured, a catch in her voice. "She doesn't understand."

"We've got to *make* her understand," Terence said grimly.

Nancy cleared her throat. "There's something else. Like I said before, inside information's being leaked out. I don't know how." She hesitated, chewing on her lower lip.

"What is it, Nancy?" Katherine asked.

"Those cars that chased us in the park were black sedans. Just like the kind that Tyler Scott and Katz drive and probably Wiggins, too, if he has one. Can that be a coincidence?"

There was a moment of stunned silence, then Terence said, "Nancy, are you suggesting that Tyler or one of his men is . . ." He let the sentence trail off. "That's impossible! Tyler's been with us for years. He's personally vouched for John Wiggins and Ray Katz and that's good enough for me."

"There are lots of black sedans," Katherine added slowly. "Those cars were rented by Mr. Scott and his men when they came to River Heights." Her brow was knit. "You said one of the sedans smashed into your friend's bumper. Surely that would dent that car's grill or bumper. Have you checked their cars for damage?"

"I've seen Tyler's and Katz's cars. They don't appear to have any damage," Nancy admitted.

"Well, let's settle this right now." Terence leaped to his feet. "Wiggins's sedan is parked at the side of the house."

Terence turned on the outside lights and they all trudged around the house. Sure enough, beside Tyler's sedan was another one. There wasn't a single dent on either the smooth black frame or chrome grill.

"I guess I was worried for nothing," Nancy said lightly, but inside she wasn't so sure. What if whoever had tried to kill her knew that Tyler's men drove black sedans? Wouldn't it be smart for them to drive black sedans, too? It certainly would confuse the issue.

Nancy kept her thoughts to herself. She'd warned the Austins and that's all that could be done.

The next morning Nancy was awakened by the telephone. Groping for the receiver, she mumbled, "Drew residence."

"Rise and shine, Nancy," a familiar male voice greeted her. "What self-respecting detective spends the morning in bed?"

"Ned!" Nancy said, delighted.

"I haven't forgotten our date Friday night," he said. "And I want to make sure River Heights doesn't drop the ball and lose this year."

Nancy stretched. "The game. Finally I can think about the game!"

"Have you been busy? Don't tell me another case has come along?"

"Come and gone. It's all over now." An uneasy thought nagged Nancy's mind, but she thrust it aside. Cindy was safe at home. That's what mattered. "What time will you be here on Friday?"

"Around noon, I hope. Maybe earlier. I have a few things I've got to finish up at school, then I'm yours for the weekend."

"Great. I'm looking forward to it."

"Don't get involved in any mystery between now and then, okay?"

"I'll try not to." She laughed. "Oh, by the way. I have one little favor to ask."

"Shoot."

"Well, there's this young girl I've met. She's twelve. Her parents are visiting River Heights and she's kind of bored. Would you mind taking her with us to the game?" Nancy's voice didn't carry a lot of enthusiasm, but she'd promised Barbara and Terence she would look out for Cindy.

"Whatever you want. Think she'll really want to see a River Heights High game?"

"She just needs to get out of the house and do something," Nancy answered.

"Okay. I'll see you Friday."

"I'll be waiting."

Nancy hung up. She hadn't had much time to herself in the last few days, so she took a leisurely shower and then got dressed.

After lunch she decided to go shopping. The game was only a couple of days away and she hadn't even thought about what she was going to wear.

She was about to leave the house, when the phone rang. Maybe it's Ned again, she thought, as she called, "I'll get it," to Hannah and snatched up the receiver in the den.

"Nancy?" a quavering voice asked.

"Barbara?" Nancy questioned. She could barely recognize the woman's voice.

"Oh, Nancy, it's terrible. Something awful has happened!"

Nancy sank into a chair. "What?"

"Cindy's run off again! She's gone! We can't find her anywhere!"

Is Cindy still playing games? Nancy wondered, as Barbara rushed on.

"We've called Lieutenant Bennington. He's here now. But I know he thinks it's all a big waste of time." Barbara's voice lowered. "Nancy, I'm scared. We really talked to Cindy last night. We told her just why it's so important that she stay home with us. She promised me she wouldn't leave again."

She's promised that before, Nancy thought grimly.

"Could you come out to the house? Please?" Barbara asked.

"Don't worry," Nancy assured her. "I'm on my way."

Half an hour later Nancy was ringing the bell at the Connellys' front door.

"Nancy!" Barbara whispered in a strained voice, opening the door. "Thank goodness you're here. It's worse than we knew. I can't tell you— it's so—" She broke off in a choking sob.

"What's worse? Has something else happened?" Nancy asked, alarmed.

"Yes." Barbara swallowed, half dragging Nancy into the house. Terence Austin was standing in a tight circle in the living room with Tyler Scott, John Wiggins, and Ray Katz. They were all sober-faced. Terence clutched a piece of paper in his hands. Wordlessly he handed it to Nancy.

In bold black print, Nancy read: We have your daughter. Don't inform the authorities. Unless you turn over the results of your research to us by nine P.M. Friday, Cindy will die. . . .

It was signed the Master.

10

Secret Formula

Nancy stared down at the ominous message, her spine tingling with dread. "A ransom note," she said, looking up.

"I found it shoved under the front door," Barbara said.

"Where's Lieutenant Bennington?" asked Nancy.

It was Tyler Scott who answered. "He left before this arrived. At least that's one piece of luck."

"Piece of luck?" Terence Austin burst out. "This is a ransom note! Cindy's really been kidnapped!"

"We don't know that for sure," Tyler said. "It could be just another clue Cindy left for Nancy."

Nancy stared down at the note. The ransom

demand sounded serious. She didn't think it was any hoax. "The kidnappers are giving you until nine Friday night to meet their demands. Why so much time? There must be a reason . . ." Then, deciding the moment had come to be direct, Nancy asked Terence, "Who is the Master?"

The Austins exchanged glances with Tyler Scott, and Nancy saw the security man almost imperceptibly shake his head.

"I've heard you speak of him before," Nancy admitted.

Barbara drew a deep breath. Ignoring Tyler's angry scowl, she said, "Nancy needs to know the truth. The Master's an enemy of our government. A foreign agent who—"

"Dr. Austin!" Tyler warned.

She whirled on him. "He's got our daughter! We have to stop him! We *need* Nancy's help!"

"We can't have Nancy Drew interfering when—" Tyler Scott began, but Terence angrily cut *him* off.

"You're talking about our child, Tyler!" he thundered. "I want Nancy's help, too."

"But if this is a real kidnapping," John Wiggins put in, "we don't have time for amateurs. I'm sorry, Miss Drew," he added as an afterthought. He walked back to the couch and sat down wearily, wincing a little as if his feet hurt.

Nancy wasn't about to be persuaded by this first sign of politeness from any of Tyler's men. "I would like to help," she said, addressing Terence Austin.

Terence ignored Tyler and said to Nancy, "We're not certain this note is truly from the Master. It could be from Cindy herself."

"Cindy knows about the Master?" asked Nancy.

Terence sighed. "I guess none of us really knows what Cindy's overheard. Sometimes she eavesdrops. I suppose it could be one of her pranks, although it's not like her to do something so deliberately cruel."

"I think you have to take this one seriously," Ray Katz broke in. "But I agree with Tyler. Involving the police is too risky."

"The note doesn't say anything about telling Nancy," Terence pointed out. "It just warns us not to tell the authorities." He looked at Nancy squarely. "I think it's time we told you everything."

Tyler gave a short bark of disbelief, then strode out of the room as if he couldn't stand to watch Terence commit such a terrible security leak. Wiggins and Katz stayed where they were, but when Terence didn't continue speaking they took the hint and followed Tyler.

Terence and Barbara sat down beside each other on the couch. Clasping his wife's hand, Terence began, "The Master is a known enemy agent. He's been the mastermind behind several international thefts of government secrets. That's why he calls himself the Master."

"You mean he's a spy?" asked Nancy.

"Yes. He's tough and ruthless and uses any means to gather information and sell it to the highest bidder. If he's got Cindy . . ."

Hearing the sick worry in his voice, Nancy quickly interrupted, "Has the Master ever threatened you before?"

"Not like this. But now our project basically is finished. Tyler thinks the Master's been waiting to make his move."

It makes sense, Nancy thought. "You said Cindy eavesdrops. Could she know something vital about your research? Something the Master wants?"

"No." Terence was positive. His brows drew into a line of concentration. "I'm going to trust you completely, Nancy, and I hope I'm not sorry. My wife and I are biochemists and our research involves very technical procedures, nothing Cindy could understand without a vast background in science—the kind of background it takes years to accumulate. Even being a child genius, Cindy couldn't begin to understand some of the procedures."

Barbara burst out, "Nancy, we're working on a formula to delay aging. Think about it! It won't be long before we can prolong life indefinitely!"

"Prolong life—*forever?*" Nancy repeated. "But that's impossible!"

"Not impossible at all," Terence said with a slight smile. "But there's a dark side too: unfriendly governments would pay a lot of money to obtain our formula."

He climbed to his feet and began pacing the room. "The Master will sell the formula to the highest bidder. If the Master has kidnapped Cindy, he did it to acquire our research, as the ransom note demands. Cindy doesn't know enough about our formula to tell him anything useful."

"Do you think we should ignore Tyler's warning and call the police anyway?" Barbara asked Terence.

Terence looked down at his hands, rubbing them together. "This is a kidnapping," he said seriously. "If we call the police, the FBI will be involved, too. The Master warned us not to call the authorities. What if he finds out and harms Cindy?"

"What should we do?" Barbara turned to Nancy.

Nancy thought hard. "I think the question is, Could the note be a hoax? Something sent by Cindy?"

They both looked so miserable Nancy was almost sorry she'd asked. Terence shook his head as if he'd come to a decision. "No, even if Cindy knows about the Master, she wouldn't let us think she'd been kidnapped." He heaved a deep sigh. "I believe the Master has her."

91

"Who was the last one to see Cindy?" Nancy asked.

Barbara answered, "Julianne. Katherine let her stay home from school today—to keep Cindy company. I'll get her."

A few minutes later she brought Julianne into the living room.

"Julianne," Nancy asked kindly. "I know you've already told everyone about when you last saw Cindy, but could you tell me, too?"

"Well, it was early this afternoon, about twelve-thirty, I guess," the girl said. "Cindy was just sitting on the porch rail. I asked her what she was doing. She said she was bored."

"Did she say anything else?"

Julianne screwed up her face in concentration. She shook her head. "No."

"Did anything else happen today? Anything unusual?"

"You mean like the phone call?"

Barbara and Terence both started. "What phone call?" Nancy asked gently.

"The one Cindy got." Realizing she'd said something important, Julianne's young face tightened up. "I didn't mean not to tell!" she cried. "I didn't know!"

"It's okay. It's okay," Nancy soothed her. "Why don't you just tell me about the phone call."

Julianne started to cry. "Well, it was—a man

92

—and he—wanted to talk—to Cindy," she said between sobs.

"You mean you answered the phone?" Nancy guessed.

She bobbed her head. "I thought it was Mr. Scott. It sounded like him."

Nancy held her breath. "Then what happened?"

"I just called Cindy. She took the phone. I left." Julianne turned tear-drenched eyes to Nancy. "I'm sorry."

"You didn't do anything wrong," Nancy assured her. Glancing at Barbara and Terence, Nancy could see their worry for Cindy's safety had grown. "Thank you, Julianne," Nancy said.

"What now?" Barbara asked in a quiet voice after Julianne had left the room.

"I think Lieutenant Bennington should be told about the ransom note," Nancy said seriously. "You need the police."

"But what about Cindy? What if the Master means what he says?" Barbara demanded.

"Either way, we only have until Friday night," Terence reminded her. He gave her a reassuring hug. "I'll call the lieutenant, but I have a feeling he won't take this much more seriously than he did Cindy's other disappearance. I don't know if I can convince him this is real."

"We're counting on you," Barbara said to Nancy.

93

"I'll do what I can," Nancy promised, a strategy forming in her mind. She'd been so intent on finding Cindy the first time, she realized that she hadn't followed up on several suggestive leads. Now she had to. And she only had two days to solve the case.

Back at home, Nancy went over the events that had happened during Cindy's first disappearance. She racked her brain to remember every detail, trying to recall those times when something had struck her as odd. She wished now that she hadn't ignored those nagging feelings as she'd dashed around searching for Cindy.

She fell asleep dreaming of muddy boots, black sedans, and a torn pants leg, and the next morning awoke with a plan.

Nancy got to the Connelly house early and was pleased to see that Tyler Scott's car was not parked outside. She asked Barbara and Terence Austin a few more questions, but she was really waiting for an opportunity to do some checking on Tyler.

While the Austins stayed near the telephone, hoping to hear from the kidnapper, Nancy slipped away. She headed for Tyler's room, the guest room on the ground floor at the back of the Connelly house.

She knocked lightly on the door. When there was no answer, she twisted the knob. The room

94

was empty. Quickly, she searched it, but found nothing useful.

Hearing car tires scrunching on gravel, Nancy glanced out the window. One of the black sedans was approaching. Nancy made a speedy exit from Tyler's room and was safely inside the Connellys' living room when Wiggins came through the front door.

Seeing Nancy, he said, "Still on the case?"

Since he'd become a little more friendly, Nancy smiled. "I guess I keep hoping that Cindy hasn't really been kidnapped. She left me a clue last time. I wish I could find one now."

Another black sedan approached, and this time Nancy saw Katz climb out of the car. But the look he sent Nancy as he stepped into the living room was far from friendly. "Is there something I can help you with?" he asked coolly.

"Well, yes, there is, as a matter of fact."

He glowered at her, but Wiggins said, "What is it?"

"Why did Tyler Scott rent black sedans for all three of you? I mean, was there a particular reason for choosing black?"

"It's what the rental company had," Katz said shortly. "We needed cars. We got them. In our business, color doesn't much matter."

"What rental company was that?" asked Nancy.

"River Heights Car Rental at the airp—" Katz

cut himself off and glared at Nancy. "Just what new lead are you following now?" he demanded.

"Oh, nothing." Nancy smiled.

"Come on," said Katz, and he and Wiggins walked outside and climbed into the same car.

As soon as they had gone, Nancy jumped into her sports car and drove directly to River Heights Car Rental at the airport. Once she explained who she was, the owner was happy to help her.

"I just want to see the records of the cars Mr. Tyler Scott rented," she informed him as he led her to his office.

"Here they are," he said, turning the book which listed their daily rentals in Nancy's direction. "Three black sedans, all the same type and make."

Nancy read the entry. "Do you have other black cars here like those?"

"Not black. But that red one over there is the same model." He pointed to a car on the lot.

Nancy shook her head. "Have any cars been turned in for repairs—any black cars like that?"

"No," he said.

Nancy had reached a dead end. Disappointed, she thanked the man for his trouble and drove home, thinking hard. The phone was ringing as she walked through her front door. "Hello?" she answered, still lost in thought about the black sedans.

There was a pause and a click. "Hurry, Nancy!" Cindy Austin's voice cried. "I need your help! I'm at the mill on the river. Don't call the police. *I know who the Master is!*"

Then the line went dead.

11

Abandoned Mill

"Hello! Cindy?" Nancy jiggled the receiver. "Cindy? Are you there?"

The line buzzed. Realizing Cindy was gone, Nancy hung up, her mind racing. She reviewed the call again. It had definitely been Cindy's voice. She'd sounded excited—almost scared. But there had been that pause and click.

Could Cindy's voice have been taped?

As Nancy thought about it she grew certain she was right. The pause and click were a dead giveaway. But had the phone call been Cindy's idea? Or the kidnapper's? Had Cindy escaped the Master's clutches? Or was it a trick? And why had she called Nancy? Why not her parents? Had there really *not* been a kidnapping? Was Cindy still playing detective?

Nancy picked up the receiver and punched out

the Connellys' number. The phone rang on and on, but there was no answer. "Great," she muttered, hanging up.

So she wouldn't forget them, she wrote down Cindy's exact words on the notepad by the phone. Biting her lip, she read them over again. She knew the abandoned mill—it was on the water near Riverfront Park. Cindy could easily have seen it when she'd visited the park or even while she'd been hiding out at Chatham Central High School.

On the other hand, the message hadn't sounded like one Cindy would give. Knowing Cindy, Nancy felt certain that if Cindy were going to send her a message, it would be in the form of a "detective test." Cindy would tease Nancy with another nursery rhyme or puzzle of some sort. This call for help was totally out of character.

The phone rang again at the same moment there was a knock at the door. "I'll be right there," Nancy called, reaching for the phone. Her pulse jumped. Maybe Cindy was calling back!

"It's us," Bess called from outside.

"Let yourselves in," Nancy yelled. "I've got to get the phone."

Bess and George walked through the door as Nancy swept up the receiver once more. "Hello?" she said breathlessly.

"Miss Drew? Hi, this is Carl, from River

Heights Car Rental at the airport. You were by earlier today."

"Yes, I was," she said, disappointed that it wasn't Cindy.

"I've got some information for you. Remember those black cars you wanted to know about? The ones Mr. Scott rented? Well, I was going through the records and I found something kind of odd."

"What?"

"Well, the next day another fellow came in and rented two black sedans. He absolutely insisted they be black. They're a little different from the ones Mr. Scott rented, but not much. Maybe it's nothing, but it just seemed kind of coincidental."

Nancy thought it was coincidental, too. "What's this man's name?"

"Lyter. Scott Lyter."

Nancy gripped the receiver more tightly. "Can you remember what Mr. Lyter looked like?"

"Well, he was tall and had dark hair. He was real serious. The kind of guy you wouldn't want to mess with. You know what I mean?"

"I know exactly what you mean. Thanks, Carl!"

Nancy hung up and snatched up her coat. She thought fast. If Cindy really was at the mill Nancy needed to get there in a hurry. However, she had a strong feeling the mill was a trap.

"I've got to go follow up on a lead," she said in sudden decision.

"A lead?" Bess asked, puzzled.

100

"Cindy's missing again, and this time the Austins received a ransom note." Nancy explained briefly about the Master, but was careful to keep the Austins' research a secret. Then she told them about Cindy's phone call, adding, "I think it was taped, though. The Master might be planning another 'accident' for me."

"Then I'm not leaving your side," George said loyally. She looked at Bess, who offered a quivering smile and said, "Me, neither."

Nancy smiled. "You guys are great." As they drove, she told them about her conversation with Carl.

"Wow, he described Tyler Scott to a T, didn't he?" Bess asked.

Nancy nodded. "But all those security men have that same look. Carl's evidence doesn't prove anything. We have to find those cars."

"How?" George asked.

"I don't know yet," Nancy admitted frankly. "Let's see if Cindy's really at the mill. If the Master has Cindy he could be using her as bait."

"Oh, Nancy, this is really getting dangerous!" Bess said fearfully.

"I know." Nancy was grim. "But even if the call is a trap, I've got to try and find Cindy."

The abandoned mill was at the end of a weed-choked lane. Nancy slowed her car to a crawl and inched forward through the trees.

"The place looks deserted," George observed.

Bess shivered. "It gives me the creeps."

"It does look deserted." Nancy turned off the engine. "Let's see if it is."

The three girls cautiously walked toward the wooden mill. The front door was ajar. A shiny new padlock hung open on the latch.

"Someone's here," Bess whispered, grabbing Nancy's arm.

There were footprints in the soft mud on the ground outside. "Bess, stay here and keep guard," said Nancy. "George and I will go inside."

"Are you kidding? Forget it. George can keep guard. I'm coming with you."

"I would rather keep a lookout, anyway," George said. "We're probably being watched."

"You could be right," Nancy admitted, and she stepped cautiously inside the darkened building.

"Ugh!" cried Bess, when a spider web brushed her face.

Nancy switched on her flashlight, sweeping it around the gloomy room. She quickly examined the area. This part of the mill was one large, empty room. A thick layer of dust covered everything.

"Those aren't Cindy's footprints," Nancy said, playing her light on the set of clear marks. "They're much too large." Carefully she followed them anyway. They led to a ladder nailed to the wall on the far end. Above the ladder was a trap door. Nancy switched off her flashlight.

"Now what?" Bess asked nervously. She glanced back to the front door.

"I'm going up."

"Don't be crazy! Someone could be up there waiting for you!"

"This is our only clue to Cindy's whereabouts," Nancy said in a low voice. "I don't have a choice."

Nancy began climbing the rungs. Several of them were broken and she had to step carefully. Before she'd climbed halfway her head was covered with cobwebs and her palms were black with dirt and dust.

She glanced down at Bess. Bess's face was a pale circle in the dark. Reaching upward, Nancy pushed on the trap door. It didn't budge. She pushed again, and it moved, showering her with more dirt.

"Yuk," she said.

"Be careful." Bess's warning drifted upward.

With a strong push Nancy heaved open the door. Something swooped past her head. A rush of wings and squeaks followed. Bats! Nancy realized, as they flapped wildly against her face.

Bess screamed. "Nancy!"

"I can't see!" Nancy cried. Suddenly her hand lost its grip. A moment later she was pitching headlong to the floor!

12

Trapped!

"Nancy!" Bess shrieked.

Nancy's hand flailed backward. She scrambled for a hold. Her hand connected with a rung and she grabbed on. The rotten wood groaned against loose nails. She closed her eyes, hoping the ladder would hold her weight.

Seconds passed. Nancy heard distant running footsteps, then more footsteps came pounding closer. Slowly, she opened her eyes. She was still on the ladder.

"What's going on?" George's voice demanded. She slowed to a stop beside Bess. "Nancy, are you all right?"

"I'll live," Nancy said, swallowing. Carefully she climbed down the ladder. At the back of the mill a door slammed.

"What was that?" Bess asked fearfully.

"*That's* whoever made the footprints. Come on!" Nancy switched on her flashlight. Her legs were shaky but she dashed in the direction of the noise. She was certain the same person who had lured her to the ladder was now trying to escape.

Bess and George were on her heels. There was a door at the end of the room. Nancy tried to open it, but it was stuck. She shoved her shoulder against the panels. It inched open. She squeezed through into another room and saw more footprints. Running forward she came to an outside door. She turned the knob and pushed. The door cracked open but was held by a strong latch. Nancy could hear running footsteps, heading around the side of the building. She pushed harder against the latch and saw a shiny new padlock holding it closed.

"Quick!" Nancy yelled to Bess and George. "Back the other way!"

Nancy ran as fast as she could through the darkened room, the yellow circle from her flashlight bobbing ahead. If they'd been padlocked in on one side, what would prevent whoever made the footprints from doing the same on the other!

She raced for the front door. George beat her to it, but the door was already closing shut! George struggled to keep it open, wedging her foot between the door and the jamb.

"I know who you are!" Nancy shouted. "So do the police!"

George was shoved inward by a large, gloved

hand. She fell backward. The door slammed with a bang. The padlock clicked shut. Nancy rammed her shoulder against the wood. The door cracked open the length of the latch. Peering through, she saw the back of a familiar figure in a dark raincoat running toward the woods. He wore a pair of black boots.

"Tyler!" she yelled. "Tyler!"

The figure disappeared through the trees.

George tried to push against the door. "Was it really Tyler?" she asked, out of breath.

"I think so. I couldn't see his face."

Bess stumbled up to them. "Are we locked in?" she asked fearfully.

Nancy shoved her shoulder against the door once more but it wouldn't budge another inch. "I'm afraid so." She sighed. "I was right. It was a trap."

"I should have stayed outside," George muttered, angry with herself. "I ran in when Bess started screaming."

"Don't blame yourself," said Nancy. "We'll just have to think about how to get out of here."

"Have any ideas?" Bess asked hopefully.

"Might as well look around as long as we're here," George suggested. "Maybe there's a way out we missed."

The three girls walked together through the abandoned building. There were no windows. What little light shone through came from cracks in the walls.

"My batteries are about gone," Nancy said as they returned to the front door. At that very moment, the flashlight beam flickered and went out.

"Oh, great." Bess slid her back down the wall and sat on the floor, discouraged. "This place is awful. It's filthy and dark and cold. We could be here forever!"

"Not forever." Nancy tried to be encouraging. "I wrote down Cindy's message on a notepad by the phone. Eventually someone will come to the mill looking for us."

George sank down beside Bess. "I hope it's before tomorrow night's game," she grumbled.

"I hope it's before tomorrow night's deadline," Nancy responded. "That's when the Austins were instructed to turn over the formula." She, too, sat down on the dusty floor, thinking hard.

They sat in silence for some time. Then Nancy picked up a piece of wood lying near the wall and tried to wedge open the door. The wood was rotten and crumbled to dust. Sighing, she said, "You know, I've been thinking. I've got this terrible feeling the man I saw running away wasn't Tyler Scott. This man was bulkier."

Bess groaned. "Who else could he be?"

"Someone I've seen before. Someone who knows my every move. I think he was the man outside Tony's."

"Could he be Wiggins or Katz?" George asked.

"Maybe, though this man appears bigger than

107

either one of them. He always wears a hat and a dark raincoat. He's obviously going to great pains to make certain I don't recognize him."

George shoved her shoulder against the door again. The padlock stayed secure. She glared at the latch, then asked, "If the Master isn't Tyler Scott, how is he keeping such a close watch on the Austins?"

"Someone on the inside is involved." Nancy chewed on her lower lip. "Wiggins and Katz aren't staying at the Connellys'. Maybe one or both of them is working for the Master. The cars might be wherever they're staying. Remind me to check on that when we get out of here."

"When we get out of here . . ." Bess leaned against the wall.

"My dad'll be calling the Connellys' to see if I'm there and—I hope—they'll start an all-out search." Nancy swiped grime from her pants. "The one thing I'm sure of now is that Cindy's really been kidnapped this time. The Master's got her and he forced her to make that tape. It wasn't Cindy who locked us in here."

"I hope she's all right," George said, sounding worried. "She's really in over her head."

"I wish she'd realized that before," Nancy murmured. "Let's take another look around. Maybe there's something above that trap door. Time's running out."

At that moment a car's engine sounded, and Nancy ran to the crack in the door, peering intently. "Someone's coming! I think it's . . . Yes, it's my dad!"

"Great!" Bess was on her feet in an instant. George tried to see through the crack, too.

"There are two of them," she remarked.

"It's Dad and Terence Austin. Dad! In here!" Nancy called. "We're all right. We're just stuck."

"Nancy!" Carson Drew exclaimed in relief. He appeared at the door, and the light from a flashlight nearly blinded them as it swept across their faces. "We saw your car and were really worried."

"We're fine. Just cold and hungry," Nancy assured him.

Terence made a sound of relief. "When your father called and asked for you, I had this terrible feeling . . ." He shuddered. "I just had to come."

"We'll get you girls out in a minute," said Carson Drew. "Who locked you in?"

"I think it was either the Master or one of his henchmen."

Dr. Austin started in surprise. "The Master?"

"I don't know for certain, but the message I had from Cindy was taped, and only the Master could have taped her voice. And no one else knew we were at the mill."

"I'll get a crowbar from my car and wrench the latch off this door," Carson Drew said. Minutes later Nancy, Bess, and George stepped into the chilly night.

"I would like to talk to both you and Barbara,"

Nancy said seriously to Terence as they walked toward where the cars were parked.

"Why don't you come to the house?" he invited.

Nancy looked at George and Bess.

"I can't go anywhere looking like this," Bess said, brushing dirt off her grimy jacket.

George winked at Nancy, then asked Carson Drew if he'd mind dropping off two bedraggled damsels.

"No trouble at all," he said with a smile. "I'll see you at home later, Nancy," he added as he and the two girls climbed into his car.

As Nancy stepped inside the Connellys' front door, she caught sight of herself in the entry hall mirror. She choked back a laugh. Her hair was covered with cobwebs and her face was smudged with dust. Her clothes had fared no better. Her navy jacket was now a dirty shade of gray.

Katherine Connelly appeared in the mirror beside her. "Terence told me about your latest adventure," she said. "Want something to eat after you wash up?"

"I'd love something," Nancy admitted.

A few minutes later, when Nancy walked into the kitchen, Katherine handed her a sandwich. "Terence said you wanted to talk to him."

"That's right. But is Tyler Scott here? I'd rather talk to the Austins without him around."

"He's with them, I'm afraid," Katherine said. "You don't trust him, do you?"

Nancy shrugged. "All I have are theories at this point."

By the time Nancy had finished her sandwich, Barbara and Terence were waiting for her in the living room. Like a black shadow, Tyler Scott stood by the fireplace, his arms crossed over his chest.

Ignoring him, Nancy said, "I want to talk about the Master. All I've heard is that he's an enemy agent who's willing to risk everything to get what he wants. What does he look like? Have any of you actually seen him?"

It was Tyler who answered. "No one's seen him, Miss Drew. He's too careful. And, as I've said before, let the professionals handle this case."

"The Master is a ruthless enemy agent," Terence put in, "but he could be anybody, or everybody. More than one person could use his name."

"I think he's just one person," Barbara said. "He's out there, waiting. And he's got my daughter."

Seeing that Barbara's control was breaking, Nancy asked quickly, "Do you think he kidnapped Cindy now because it was convenient?"

"Yes." Again Tyler answered. "The idea was planted in his head by Cindy's antics. It was so easy. Cindy was bored and looking for a way to escape. He found an opportunity to kidnap her and took it."

Tyler's theories so closely agreed with Nancy's that she decided to take a chance. "Do you know anything about a man calling himself Scott Lyter?" she asked him.

"Scott Lyter?" He gave her an odd look, his eyes frosty. "No," he said flatly.

Nancy's skin prickled. He was lying! She was sure of it!

Terence looked puzzled by this change of topic. "Who's Scott Lyter?"

"Just a lead I followed that didn't really pan out," Nancy murmured.

Sensing there was nothing more she could do, Nancy walked out into the October night. She stood on the porch and took a deep breath. The rain had cleared and a faint moon showed through the trees. Glad no one had parked behind her, Nancy was on her way to her car when she saw Tyler Scott's silhouette move by the window. He's watching me, she thought, as if he wants to make sure I leave. She opened her car door and slid behind the wheel.

Tyler turned away from the window. Nancy backed out of the driveway, drove a few yards down the road, then parked, got out and doubled back. She didn't know what she expected to learn but she had to take a chance.

She walked around to the back of the house. A light shone in Tyler's room, and the window was raised slightly. Nancy peered inside, but the room was empty.

She waited in the shadows of the bushes, wondering if she should confront Tyler. A door slammed, and she heard a car engine start up. Still she waited.

Nancy was about to give up her vigil when Wiggins walked into Tyler's room. He rubbed his jaw and looked worried. Nancy held her breath. She'd never seen him show any emotion whatsoever.

Suddenly he whirled around, facing the hallway. "Wait a minute, Katz," he muttered, looking around as if he didn't want anyone else to hear. Nancy edged closer to the window, but she still couldn't see into the hallway. Wiggins's next words chillingly confirmed her suspicions.

"I overheard that Drew girl talking to Tyler about a *Scott Lyter!* How did she get Tyler's alias? *And what kind of game is Tyler playing?*"

13

Turning the Tables

The next day the familiar car pulling into the Drews' driveway had Nancy racing to the door. "Ned!" she called, excited.

Ned Nickerson unfolded his long legs from the front seat. He grinned at her, his brown hair tossed by the wind. Nancy was so glad to see his solid, athletic form that she raced down the walk to his car.

He pulled a small pennant on a stick from his dashboard and waved it at her. It was a River Heights High pennant. "Rah, rah, and all that," he greeted her. "The time has come to cage the Wildcats."

"I'm so glad you're here!" Nancy exclaimed. She practically dragged Ned inside the house.

"Don't tell me you're wearing that to the

game," he said, eyeing her sweatshirt and paint-spattered jeans.

"It's been a tough week. This is about the extent of my wardrobe these days," Nancy replied, grinning. It was so good to see Ned again. "Don't worry," she told him. "I'll be ready in time."

"What happened to your clothes?"

"Sit down," she said, guiding him to the sofa. "I've got a lot to tell you and time is running out! I have to figure out where Tyler has Cindy hidden before nine tonight!"

"Whoa! How about starting at the beginning?"

She settled beside him on the couch. "Okay, I'll tell you everything that happened from the first moment I met Cindy Austin."

"Well," Ned said, somewhat dazed, when Nancy had finished. "And here I thought we were just going to a game tonight."

Nancy stared off into space. "You know, telling you this has really helped me. I just thought of something."

"What?"

"Tyler's had one of his men following me everywhere. I've never been able to figure out how. But now I've got an idea!"

She was out the door before Ned could even ask her what she meant. He followed after her to find her lying on her back beneath her car.

"What are you looking for?"

She didn't answer him. Ned waited patiently as Nancy next searched the interior of her car, running her hands beneath the seats and dashboard. With the look of determined concentration Ned had seen many times before, Nancy finally searched in the trunk.

"Did you find anything?" Ned asked.

"No." Disappointed, she shut the trunk. She stood still for a moment, biting into her lower lip. She glanced at the car, then bent down and ran her hand inside the bumper. "Aha!" she cried triumphantly, holding out a small metal disk.

Ned's brows raised. "A homing device?"

"Right! I knew there had to be a way the Master kept such close track of me." Nancy turned the small disk over in her hand, then carefully put it back. "Let's not tip our hand yet," she said. "I've got to call George right away."

Nancy dashed back in the house and placed the call. "George," she said excitedly when her friend answered. "Check your parents' station wagon. There might be a homing device in the back bumper."

"But the back bumper was replaced when we got the car fixed," George said.

"They might have replaced the device, George," Nancy said. "Check the station wagon anyway. Okay?"

"Okay. I'll call you back if I find anything."

"Well?" Ned asked, once Nancy was off the phone.

"George is going to call back. In the meantime this explains a lot of things." She paced across the room. "But I haven't noticed anyone following me so closely lately," she said to herself. "I think they've backed off. Tyler must be afraid I'll catch on to him."

The phone rang and Nancy snatched up the receiver. "I found it!" George cried excitedly. "It was in the front bumper."

"That's how they trapped us at the park. I'll bet they planted that device on your car when you picked me up at the Connellys' the night my car was towed. They must be really fast. You and Bess were only away from the car a few minutes."

"That means whoever did it was at the house that night!"

"Right." Nancy grew sober.

"Are you going to the game tonight, Nancy?" George asked. "Or will you be with the Austins?"

"I don't know," Nancy admitted. "I may not have a choice. Ned's here and I think he'd wring my neck if he thought I wasn't going to the game."

"Well, Bess and I'll be there. Try to find us if you come."

"Will do."

Nancy hung up and turned to Ned. "There are some things I've got to do today before the game."

"Like what? What are you thinking about?" Ned asked, seeing the faraway look in Nancy's blue eyes.

"If you wanted to throw suspicion on someone, how would you do it?" Before Ned could answer, Nancy continued, "You might manufacture evidence to make it look as if he'd committed the crime. Then you'd fade into the background yourself, right?"

Ned smiled at her. "You're on to something, aren't you?"

"Maybe. I don't know yet."

"What do you want to do?"

"In case someone's watching, let's leave the house and act like nothing's happened. Talk about the game or something. When we come out, I'll get in my car and you get in yours."

"And?" Ned asked.

"And . . . whoever's watching will follow me. I think it's high time we turned the tables on the Master, don't you?" Nancy said with a smile.

Catching on to her plan, Ned walked with Nancy out the front door of her house. In a loud voice, he announced, "If Chatham Central beats River Heights this year, I'm really going to give those guys on the team a bad time."

The street seemed empty but Nancy wasn't taking any chances. "I understand the Wildcats are really tough."

"Hey, they said the same thing last year and we beat them, didn't we?"

118

Nancy closed the front door behind them. No cars came down the street.

"I'll bet they're just around the corner," she said, very softly. "When I leave I'll drive to that lookout spot on the cliff above Riverfront Park. I want you to follow me, but give me lots of time. We don't want you to get ahead of our friends."

"Okay, then what?"

"You park down below, out of sight. I'll meet you there."

"How about if I park in that turnaround near the highway? You can climb down the trail and meet me."

"Perfect." Nancy smiled. It was great how well she and Ned worked together.

Ned climbed in his car and drove away, as if he were heading home. Nancy followed in her car, but meandered to the city limits. She hoped to catch sight of the Master or one of his henchmen in her rearview mirror but no black sedan moved up on her.

She drove leisurely toward the cliffside, checking her watch from time to time. Ned had promised to give her a lot of time but she didn't want to chance having him meet the Master.

The lookout spot was remote and high above the river. Nancy had a bird's-eye view. She could see the green acres of the park on one side, the buildings and streets of River Heights on the other.

She sat in the car and waited, her eyes constantly searching her rearview mirror. She could see a long way down the winding road that led to the clifftop. The Master wouldn't be able to get by her.

What if he doesn't follow? she fretted uneasily as the minutes passed. He hadn't followed her when she'd gone to the school in search of Cindy. He might not be tracking her all the time.

Just as she was certain she'd wasted her time, a black sedan began slowly climbing the winding road far below. Heart beating rapidly, Nancy slipped out of the driver's seat and hid behind a screen of bushes. She didn't waste time. Running down the slippery hillside trail, she raced to meet Ned. She had to reach him before the black sedan doubled back.

Branches and thorns ripped her jacket and tore at her hair. Dirt spilled into the tops of her running shoes. Nancy didn't care. She had to get to Ned.

With a cry of relief she came to the small turnaround. Ned's car was hidden from the main road. He waved to Nancy as she staggered from the trail.

Climbing in beside him, she asked anxiously, "Have they come down yet?"

"Nope." He gave her a sidelong look. "You've got stickers in your hair."

"I know, I—there they are!" she cried.

The black sedan was heading at a fast clip down the highway. Ned waited a few moments then pulled smoothly out behind them. He kept back as far as he dared.

"Can you see them?" he asked as he put on a little more speed.

"They're way ahead. A black dot. Oh, wait, they're turning! Hurry! Hurry!"

Ned pressed on the accelerator. They reached the road the sedan had turned onto. It was Kingsman Road.

"Chatham Central's right there." Nancy pointed. "What are they doing?"

"Wait, they're going farther. Toward that residential district."

Ned kept his distance from the black sedan. It slowed at one of the cross streets, turning into the residential district. Carefully, Ned followed.

"They've got Cindy in one of these houses," Nancy said under her breath. "I just know it!"

The black sedan disappeared at the end of the street. Ned drove after it. "It's starting to get dark," he muttered as he turned the corner.

Nancy checked her watch. There wasn't much time left. "Where did they go?" she asked, worried. The street in front of them was empty. The sedan was gone!

"There," Ned said softly, as they passed a gray house. The automatic garage door was just closing. Inside was a black sedan, its nose pointed outward. Nancy could see the dented grill.

"That's the car that smashed into us!" Nancy said, holding back her excitement.

Ned drove to the end of the street and Nancy said, "Go to the police station and tell Lieutenant Bennington what we found. I'm going after Cindy."

"What? No way! I'm not leaving you here."

"Ned, you've got to! There's no time to wait for the police. We've got to help Cindy now."

"Then you go to the police station," he argued. "I'll find Cindy."

"Ned, if Cindy's in there, she won't know who you are. She won't trust you. She *knows* me."

Ned struggled with himself. He didn't like the plan but he could see the logic in it. "Okay," he said grudgingly. "But be careful."

Nancy was already sliding out of the car. She gave Ned a thumbs-up signal, then slipped into the gathering gloom. Lights were coming on in the surrounding houses. Nancy walked slowly up the street. Running would only draw attention to her. She wanted to make certain she didn't alert the Master to her presence.

The Master. Excitement burned inside her. Nancy had the uncanny feeling she was about to find out who he was.

The gray house was still dark, except for a faint glow shining out the back. Circling the garage, Nancy saw that the light was coming from a basement window. The curtains were drawn but she could see through a faint crack. Her pulse leaped. Cindy Austin was sitting on a couch!

Nancy leaned forward to get a better look. Cindy was bound and gagged!

A hand suddenly clamped over Nancy's mouth, muffling her startled cry.

"Don't move, Miss Drew," a familiar voice warned softly. The barrel of a gun was thrust into her back. "That is if you want to live to see tomorrow."

14

The Master

Nancy didn't have to turn around to know who held her. "You're the Master, aren't you, Mr. Wiggins?" she said against his fingers.

She felt his surprise. Slowly he removed his hand, but the gun was still pressed hard against her shoulder blades. "So you figured it out," he said. "I wondered if you would."

"It had to be either you or Tyler Scott or Katz," Nancy said calmly. "As soon as I realized someone was leaking information I knew the traitor had to be someone on the inside. I thought it was Tyler, but the clues pointing to him were just too convenient. You made sure of that."

Wiggins chuckled harshly. "It was so easy. You wanted to believe it was Tyler because he was so nasty to you."

"That's true," Nancy admitted. "You even

made it look like you were talking to Katz in the hallway last night, but you weren't. It was all a setup. Another reason for me to suspect Tyler. But you're really the one who used the Scott Lyter alias."

"That's right."

"Unscramble Lyter and you've got Tyler. Scott Tyler. Tyler Scott."

He put pressure on her arm and started half leading, half dragging her to the house. Nancy glanced around desperately for Ned, but it was too soon to expect him back with the police. She had to keep Wiggins talking.

"Tyler knew that someone was using his name as an alias. That's why he reacted when I brought it up." Nancy twisted around to see Wiggins's face. "He suspects the person using Scott Lyter is the Master, doesn't he?"

The Master smiled one of the coldest smiles Nancy had ever seen. "Clever, aren't you?"

"You gave yourself away, you know."

"Oh? How's that?" He sounded almost bored.

"You were the one who found me unconscious at Mr. Carver's farm. That's when I first grew suspicious. Tyler Scott said he'd purposely sent you to watch out for me. You used that opportunity to push me into the electric fence!"

Wiggins shoved Nancy inside the back door of the gray house. She tumbled against the wall. Struggling to her feet, she stared into his hard eyes, trying to ignore the gun he had trained on

125

her. Hiding her fear, Nancy said, "If you were really looking out for me that day, you would have come forward and shown yourself right from the start. You were just waiting for a chance to get me out of the way. You even put on Mr. Carver's black rubber boots to make certain there was nothing about you I could recognize later."

"In my business you have to be more than careful, Miss Drew. You have to be perfect."

Nancy's heart was pounding furiously. "You didn't count on being bitten by the Dobermans," she said. "Your limp was the real giveaway. I didn't make the connection at first. I just thought your feet hurt. But it's your leg that's injured, isn't it?"

"Keep walking." He gestured to the dimly lit stairway to the basement.

"You were the one who moved the Detour sign and you've been following me. You put a homing device in my car and in George's."

"And your father's," he admitted. "Just to be safe."

"Then you disguised yourself with a bulky raincoat and hat so I wouldn't recognize you."

"Sometimes it was one of my men," he corrected her. "I couldn't be with you all the time. You weren't that important."

"But you were in one of the cars that tried to crush me at the park."

This time his smile was full of satisfaction. "The back car. You should have learned a lesson

126

there. Now I'm afraid your curiosity has landed you in a lot more trouble."

Nancy took several steps downward. Her throat was dry. She had to stall for time! "Tell me, how did you kidnap Cindy?"

"That was almost too easy," he bragged. "I made the phone call to implicate Tyler. And when Julianne answered, she thought I *was* Tyler. I didn't even have to lie. I fed Cindy a lot of Tyler talk and suggested strongly that she stay inside the house. I knew she'd do the opposite of what Tyler suggested. Sure enough, when I drove up, she was sitting on the porch, bored." He laughed. "I told Cindy *you* wanted to play a detective game with her and that I would take her to you. She could hardly wait to get in the car with me."

Nancy felt sick at the way he'd used Cindy. He'd known the girl's weakness for wanting to best Nancy and had taken advantage of it. "Is Katz involved, too?"

Wiggins snorted. "Katz is a rank amateur, just like Tyler Scott. Neither one of them ever suspected me. My references are impeccable and I've done my share to help maintain security."

"Oh, sure. You've done just enough to make sure everyone thinks you're a model employee," Nancy said.

"Come on, Miss Drew. You're wasting time. *Move!*"

Nancy was forced down the rest of the stairs.

Cindy stared up at her through terrified eyes. There was another man seated in a chair in front of a TV set. He stood up respectfully when Wiggins entered the room. He, too, had the same build and air of hard professionalism about him that Tyler Scott, Katz, and Wiggins possessed.

"Tie her up," Wiggins said, giving Nancy a shove that sent her sprawling on the floor.

Cindy made a sound of despair. Needing to reassure her, Nancy climbed to her feet, meeting Wiggins's cold stare courageously. "There's something I would like to know," Nancy said as calmly as she could. "How come you or one of your men didn't follow me the night I found Cindy?"

The other man grabbed Nancy's hands and jerked them behind her back. Quickly he wound a nylon rope tightly around her wrists.

"That was an unexpected piece of luck for you," Wiggins said in disgust. *"Tyler,"* he stressed with extreme dislike, "felt it was necessary that I search for Cindy with him that night." He threw a withering look at the other man. "And my men didn't take the threat of you finding Cindy seriously enough to watch you every minute."

The man finished tying Nancy's hands and pushed her onto the couch beside Cindy. If Wiggins's comments bothered him he gave no sign of it.

Nancy wished she could check her watch. How

long had it been since she'd left Ned? Half an hour? Longer? She had to keep stalling. "You made mistakes. Any amateur could have found you. It won't be long until Lieutenant Bennington catches you."

Wiggins started to laugh. His laughter rang out in the room and sent chills up Nancy's spine. "Don't hold your breath waiting for the police. They're sitting on their hands waiting for the Master to send another message. The Austins— with a lot of persuasion from Tyler"—he laughed again—"decided not to tell the police about the telephone call they got a little while ago, arranging for the transfer of their formula."

There was a sound at the top of the stairs and Wiggins's cold smile grew even colder. "Unless of course you think they might be on their way to rescue you," he added mockingly.

Feet thudded down the stairs. A huge stone-faced man appeared. Nancy gasped as she saw what he held in his arms. Ned's unconscious body was dumped on the floor at Nancy's feet!

"What have you done to him?" Nancy cried.

The Master's laughter sounded again. "He's all right. I have a man watching the street. He saw you get out of the car and he radioed me. Then he tracked your boyfriend. We couldn't have him telling all to Lieutenant Bennington, now could we?"

He checked his watch and said, "It's almost time. Sorry I have to leave you, now. Steve can keep you company." He signaled the man who'd brought Ned in, and they left together.

The man named Steve pulled a roll of tape from the pocket of his jacket and peeled off a strip. "I think you've talked enough," he said, strapping the tape firmly across Nancy's mouth.

Nancy broke out into a cold sweat. The Master had given himself away. He'd revealed his identity to both her and Cindy. They knew he was guilty of kidnapping and attempted murder. His words floated across her mind: *In my business you have to be more than careful, Miss Drew. You have to be perfect.*

Nancy didn't kid herself that he'd confessed by accident. She knew her life, Ned's, and Cindy's weren't worth much now. She had to escape!

Anxiously, her eyes searched the room for some means to free herself. There was a fireplace near her with a stone hearth. The only furniture was the couch she was sitting on, several chairs, a table with an unlit lamp, and the television set. There were no tools or knickknacks of any kind. She couldn't see anything she could use to cut through her bindings.

She looked around again. There was a nearly overflowing garbage can sitting against the wall about halfway between Nancy and her captor, Steve. Nancy stared at it. Was it her imagination or was there some kind of metal sticking out near the top? She slid to the edge of the couch and peered forward. It was the lid of a can, she realized with jubilation. But how could she get her hands on it?

Nancy glanced at Cindy. She tried to convey what she was thinking by jerking her head in the direction of the garbage sack, then wriggling her fingers. Cindy was quick to understand. To Nancy's surprise the young girl suddenly stood up, hopped forward several times, then toppled over onto the floor taking the garbage sack with her!

"Hey!" Steve yelled. He ran over to Cindy, scooping her up. Garbage was all over the floor. The lid from a tuna can was near enough to Nancy's foot for her to quickly put her shoe on it.

"What do you think you're doing?" Steve demanded furiously, shoving Cindy onto the couch. "Don't move again," he commanded, and the threat in his voice made Cindy shrink back against the cushions.

Nancy's pulse was racing. Steve settled himself back on the chair but kept glancing back at Nancy and Cindy from time to time. Ned lay to one side, his breathing regular, a bruise forming on the side of his jaw.

Slowly Nancy inched the tuna lid her way. Whenever she felt Steve's eyes on her she stopped what she was doing and looked down with concern at Ned, as if her thoughts were on him alone. Satisfied, Steve would turn back to the TV set.

Finally the lid was right next to the couch.

Nancy turned sideways. All she had to do was bend down and pick up the lid. She waited for the right moment, her heart pounding out the seconds. She was running out of time.

In her mind she counted how many seconds passed before Steve glanced their way. She realized he was checking on them about every half a minute. She wished he would get absorbed in the television program.

Across the TV screen a familiar face suddenly showed. It was Cindy's! Steve grunted in surprise as the announcer said, ". . . twelve-year-old Cindy Austin has been missing for two days. Police are searching the River Heights area. If you have any information, please call this number . . ."

Quick as a flash Nancy bent down and retrieved the tuna lid. Steve glanced her way but Nancy pretended to be trying to help Ned. At that moment Ned groaned and moved his head.

"Sit up!" Steve commanded, and Nancy jerked backward, looking frightened. As soon as he turned around again Nancy gave Cindy a quick wink.

Carefully she moved the lid between her fingers. She gripped it hard, sawing against her nylon bindings. It was painstaking work and her hands cramped. She agonized over how long it took. Time felt as if it was speeding up and she was slowing down.

Just when she was about to give up, the first

rope fell away. The bindings loosened. Quickly Nancy eased her hands free.

"Hey—what's going on?" Steve demanded, jumping to his feet, his eyes on the frayed ropes dangling from Nancy's wrists.

Nancy didn't have time to waste. She grabbed the lamp from the table. Steve charged forward. Nancy swung the lamp, but Steve's foot got tangled in the cord. He stumbled over Ned and fell. His head hit the hearth with a crack. He lay still.

Nancy ripped the tape off her mouth. She ran to Steve and felt for a pulse. His heartbeat was sound and steady. "He's just knocked out," she said breathlessly to Cindy. "We've got to hurry."

She cut through Cindy's cords and pulled the tape from her mouth. Instantly Cindy started crying. "I was so scared! I thought they were going to kill me! They made me make that phone message for you! I couldn't even call you. They were afraid I would give this place away!"

"Shhh. Help me with Ned. Come on, there might be others outside."

Carefully, Nancy moved Ned's jaw back and forth. His eyelids flickered. "Nancy?" he asked thickly.

"Are you all right, Ned?"

"My head." He groaned again and lifted a hand to his temple. "What happened?"

"The Master was waiting for us. I'll explain later. We've got to get out of here."

Ned sat up and looked around groggily. He stumbled trying to get to his feet, and Nancy put her arm around him. "Are you sure you're all right?" she asked anxiously.

"No worse than a football tackle." He grinned lopsidedly. "What about the game?"

"What game?" Cindy asked.

"Never mind." Nancy urged Ned toward the door. "Come on. Hurry." They helped Ned up the stairs. In the inky darkness Nancy asked, "What about the car? Do you know what happened to it?"

"I'm not sure. The street was blocked and I had to stop, and suddenly this guy appeared out of nowhere. He hit me and that's all I remember."

"Where was the street blocked?"

Ned pointed. "That way."

Nancy and Cindy stood on each side of him. With every step his balance grew more steady. Nancy kept glancing around. She remembered the Master had said the street was watched but she could see no one anywhere.

"There it is," Ned said with relief.

His car was parked at the corner, under a streetlight. The driver's door was unlocked.

"What about the keys?" Nancy asked. They weren't in the ignition.

"Never mind. I've got spares hidden in the dash." He leaned across the front seat and searched with his hand. Soon he handed Nancy two keys which had been taped beneath the steering wheel.

"I'll drive," Nancy said. Cindy climbed in the back and Ned sank into the passenger seat.

Nancy tried the keys. To her relief the engine started with a purr. One hand closing her door, she started to nose the car into the road.

A man's hand suddenly darted into the car, grabbing Nancy's shoulder. Cindy screamed.

"Nancy!" Ned yelled.

Nancy pressed her foot to the accelerator and the car surged forward. The man still clung to the open door! Nancy glanced at him. It was Steve. His face was full of determination. His eyes were full of fury. Though the car was speeding up, he began to pull himself inside!

15

Touchdown

"Nancy!" Cindy screamed.

Nancy whipped the wheel around. Steve yelled at her. His fingers grabbed her arm. Nancy gunned the accelerator again. Ned's hand suddenly reached out and yanked the steering wheel his way. The car spun to the right and Steve's hand lost its grip. He howled as he was hurled from the car. The car tore forward. Nancy looked back. Steve rolled to the side of the road and staggered to his feet.

She breathed a sigh of relief.

"Fancy driving, Drew," said Ned.

"Thanks to you." Nancy managed a smile.

From the backseat Nancy heard sniffling. "It's all my fault," Cindy moaned. "All of it. If I hadn't run away none of this would have happened."

"This might have happened anyway," Nancy

assured her. In spite of the anguish Cindy had caused her parents, Nancy couldn't let her blame herself for everything. "The Master was just waiting for a chance to get his hands on your parents' formula."

"But my running away gave him the idea!" Cindy wailed. "It's all my fault."

"Cindy, it's no one's fault. There's still a chance we can stop your parents from turning over the formula. We need to let them know you're okay."

"They're going to be really mad." She sniffed even more loudly.

"Believe me, they're going to be really *glad*— to see you." Nancy glanced back at her. "Cindy, did you overhear anything while you were captured? Anything that could help us stop the ransom drop?"

Cindy wiped her eyes on her sleeve. She shook her head. "I—I don't know."

"Come on, Cindy. Think." Nancy coaxed. "Did you hear any of the Master's plans? Anything at all?"

"I think he said he was meeting Tyler," she said hesitantly. "Yeah, that's right. He was laughing and laughing, like it was a big joke."

"He's meeting Tyler tonight for the drop? That doesn't make sense. Tyler thinks he and Wiggins are on the same side, and the Master would never reveal his identity unless he had to."

"No, wait!" Cindy's face cleared. "That's it!

He said something about being the hero of the team. He volunteered to turn over the formula!"

Nancy drove as fast as she dared toward the Connelly house. "I get it. Tyler thinks Wiggins is putting his life on the line by volunteering to meet one of the Master's men. But Wiggins is the Master. He's making sure nothing goes wrong. He wants that formula. We've got to find Tyler and tell him Wiggins's true identity before it's too late."

"It might already be too late," Ned put in soberly as they bumped up the Connellys' driveway. "There're no cars here."

Nancy raced to the house and pounded on the door. "Katherine! Barbara! Terence!" she called. There was no answer. "They must be waiting at the police station," she said desperately. "Let's go."

"I'll drive," said Ned, sliding behind the wheel.

"Are you sure you're all right?" Nancy asked anxiously.

"Never better." He drove them back toward the city center, maneuvering through the thick evening traffic. "There're sure a lot of cars out tonight," he grumbled. "Everybody's going to the game."

"The game?" Cindy said. "Oh! That's the Chatham Central game with River Heights. I remember now, the kids at Chatham Central were all talking about it—" She sucked in a breath. "Nancy, that's it! Wiggins—the Master —said something about the game. That's what he meant about being a hero for the team!"

A quick mental image of Wiggins's amusement crossed Nancy's mind. She could almost hear his cold laughter again—the Master's cold laughter. He'd been acting as if he'd played a spectacular joke on someone. And that joke was on *her!*

"The drop's going to be made right under all our noses," she said with dawning realization. "He's going to do it at the game! Quick, Ned, turn around. We don't have time to see the police. We've got to get to the game!"

Ned didn't waste time. He made a quick turn, and they took off in the direction of Kingsman Road and Moffett Way.

Cindy leaned forward. "He kept making remarks about me hiding out at the high school," she recalled. "He thought it was really funny, and he was really mad that you found me first."

"He's got a twisted sense of humor," Nancy said grimly. "He's using your idea to steal the formula!"

The football field's floodlights could be seen from blocks away. As they neared the stadium Nancy heard the dull roar of cheering voices.

Nancy, Ned, and Cindy dashed toward the gate.

"Now what?" Ned asked, once they were inside.

Nancy glanced around. A sea of people was

moving into the stands. The field was as bright as day. The band was playing a rousing fight song. Nancy caught a glimpse of green and gold as the Chatham Central cheerleaders leaped through a routine. "We've got to find him," she muttered.

"We'll have to split up," said Ned. "I'll go this way and circle the field. You and Cindy head that way."

"If you see Bess and George, tell them what's going on."

Ned sent her the okay signal and disappeared around one side of the stadium. Nancy and Cindy began to circle the field in the opposite direction.

"What'll we do if we find him?" Cindy asked fearfully. She kept right at Nancy's side as if seeking protection.

"We'll have to stop him." Nancy half smiled. "That's part of being a detective."

"But he'll recognize us. We'll never catch him then!"

That thought had occurred to Nancy, too. It would be better to be in disguise but there wasn't time.

"Hi, Nancy!" Christine O'Callaghan said with a bright smile. She'd separated from the cheerleaders and was buying herself a soda. A fierce Wildcat snarled at them from the front of her sweater. "Ready to get pounced?"

Nancy grabbed her arm. "Chris, I'm in the middle of a case and I need your help."

140

"Well, sure." Christine was delighted. "What can I do?"

"Change clothes with me."

"What? You want to wear a Chatham Central cheerleading outfit?" Christine looked at Nancy as if Nancy had lost her mind.

"I don't have time to explain. Will you do it?"

Christine's mouth dropped open. "Well—sure—I guess so. How will you know the routines?"

"I'll wing it," Nancy muttered, and followed Christine toward the dressing rooms.

Nancy and Christine quickly exchanged clothes. When Cindy tried to tag along after her, Nancy said, "Stay back out of sight. I don't want you to get hurt."

"But I want to help."

"You'll help me more if you just keep your eyes peeled."

"She can stay with me," Christine offered.

"Great." Cindy made a face but didn't argue.

A whistle blew and Nancy ran out to the field. The other Chatham Central cheerleaders looked at her in surprise as the two teams positioned themselves for the kickoff. Nancy searched the visiting team's bleachers for Bess and George but couldn't see them. There were too many people. Wishing she had her binoculars, Nancy tried to remember what Wiggins had been wearing. A gray jacket and dark pants, she thought.

141

At that moment Nancy saw Ned at the far end of the field, walking behind the goalposts. His attention was directed on someone in front of him. Nancy's heart leaped. It was the man who'd left with Wiggins!

Instantly Nancy melted closer to the small band of cheerleaders. The Master had to be nearby. This man must be the one who was supposedly picking up the drop.

Someone tapped Nancy on the shoulder, and she nearly jumped out of her skin. "You ready to do a cheer?" one of the Chatham Central cheerleaders asked dubiously.

"Uh . . . no . . ." Nancy half laughed. "I don't think so."

"Where's Chris?"

"She'll be back. Sorry. I've got to go . . ." Nancy's eyes were on the man Ned was following. She swept her gaze over the surrounding crowd. *There he is!* she thought triumphantly, seeing Wiggins at the edge of the home team bleachers, a thick folder under one arm.

The Austins' secret formula!

To Nancy's dismay, Wiggins started walking straight toward her. The other cheerleaders were banding together at the edge of the field. Nancy turned on her heel to join them.

"Who's going to win tonight?" one of them yelled.

"The Wildcats!" the crowd yelled back.

The cheerleaders picked up their pom-poms.

Her heart in her throat, Nancy picked up Christine's. She tried desperately to be part of the group.

Wiggins came forward. He passed within inches of Nancy's shoulder. She held her breath. He didn't even look at her.

Nancy waited a moment then followed after him. The Chatham Central cheerleaders looked at each other in bafflement, then promptly broke into another cheer.

Picking up Wiggins's trail, Nancy threaded her way through the crowd. Ned was still following the other man. Hoping Wiggins didn't see him, Nancy tried to think of some kind of plan to stop Wiggins from making the drop. Whatever happened, the exchange of the Austins' formula could not take place.

She wondered where Tyler Scott and Lieutenant Bennington were. Watching from the sidelines, she supposed. Making certain nothing went wrong until Cindy was safe.

Wiggins circled around the River Heights goalpost. His henchman came the other way. They stood by each other for a few moments as if watching the game. In the crowd behind, Ned stood, waiting.

The manila folder was still under Wiggins's arm. Nancy had a moment of crystal clear insight. The folder was a fake! Wiggins would never hand over the real formula. It was too risky. Better to stash the original somewhere and pass a fake.

Then if the authorities caught his accomplice, they would think he had somehow exchanged the original for innocent papers. And they probably couldn't even hold him as a kidnapper.

Nancy could see the faint smile on Wiggins's face—the Master's smile. He was really enjoying the joke on her, Tyler Scott, and the Austins.

Wiggins handed the folder to the other man. Just as soon as the transfer was made Nancy yelled, "Now, Ned!" at the top of her lungs.

Wiggins looked around sharply. He saw Ned and tore off in Nancy's direction. He was moving so fast he ran straight into her, pushing her down.

"Ooof!" Nancy groaned. She twisted and caught her leg around his knee, tripping him. He fell down hard.

"You!" he exclaimed.

He leaped to his feet with an athletic ability that surprised Nancy, pushing his way through the crowd. Nancy followed hot on his heels. She wouldn't let him get away!

Wiggins darted up the stadium steps, shoving Chatham Central fans out of the way. "Hey!" somebody yelled, but Wiggins kept running.

Nancy followed after him. Her heart was beating like mad, and her breath came in gasps. He wasn't going to outdistance her. He wasn't!

Suddenly a woman carrying a stroller was in Nancy's way. Nancy couldn't get around her. By the time Nancy found an opening Wiggins was at the other end of the bleachers, heading down.

"Stop him!" Nancy cried. "Stop that man!"

The crowd suddenly surged to its feet with a roar. "Touchdown!" the announcer yelled over the loudspeaker. "The Wildcats have just scored a touchdown!"

No one heard Nancy's shout. Wiggins was heading for an exit. He was getting away!

Nancy jockeyed her way through the crowd. Soon Wiggins would be out of sight. She was fighting to get to the bottom of the stadium when she suddenly saw Cindy, blocking the exit.

Cindy's face was white as she stared into the Master's. He brutally shoved her aside.

"Cindy!" Nancy screamed, pushing her way toward her.

The Master started down the steps. Cindy's arms wrapped around his leg. She clung on tightly, her eyes squinched shut.

"Let go!" the Master roared, but she hung on.

Nancy burst through the crowd and made a flying leap for Wiggins's back. She wrapped her arms around his neck, dragging him down. His fingers pried at her wrists.

"Hang on, Cindy!" she cried. "Hold him!"

"Okay, everybody stay still." Tyler Scott's voice cut through the night like a bullet.

Nancy looked up. Wiggins froze. Tyler's fingers were wrapped around a deadly-looking gun. He was aiming it directly at Wiggins's chest.

While Wiggins slowly lifted his hands to surrender, Lieutenant Bennington and police officers appeared behind him. Nancy and Cindy released Wiggins.

"Well, it's about time you got here," Wiggins said. "Nancy Drew's got some crazy idea that I'm involved, but as you can see, I rescued Cindy, safe and sound."

All the time he was speaking he was edging toward the stairway rail.

"That's a lie!" Cindy shouted. "Nancy saved me. And Nancy caught him!" She pointed an angry finger at Wiggins. "He's the Master, Tyler. He's the one who kidnapped me!"

Before Wiggins could make another move, Lieutenant Bennington calmly slipped a pair of handcuffs over the spy's wrists.

Tyler stared directly at the man he'd once considered a friend and ally. "We've caught your man," he said flatly. "He didn't have the formula on him."

"I don't know what you're talking about," Wiggins blustered.

"Try Mr. Wiggins's black sedan," Nancy suggested. "He probably hid the formula somewhere inside it before the fake handoff, since he didn't have time to stash it somewhere else."

Wiggins glared at Nancy. The Master's cold smile curved his lips. "It's not over yet, Miss Drew," he said. "We'll meet again sometime."

"Not for about twenty years or so," Lieutenant Bennington snapped. "Let's go."

Nancy watched them lead Wiggins away. Tyler Scott turned to her and frowned. It took him several tries, but he finally said, "I was wrong about you. When I'm wrong, I say so. You're an excellent detective, Nancy Drew."

"Thank you." Nancy felt a blush creep up her neck. After all his criticism, she was ill-prepared for a compliment from Tyler Scott.

One of Lieutenant Bennington's men signaled from the parking lot. They'd found the formula!

"Cindy! Cindy!" Barbara and Terence Austin came rushing up the steps toward them as Tyler Scott and Lieutenant Bennington left. With a sob of relief Cindy raced down and was swept into their waiting arms.

"I'm sorry," she murmured over and over again, hugging her parents. "I'm so sorry."

"It's all right, sweetheart," Barbara said, her eyes bright with unshed tears. "We're just glad to have you back."

"I never really thought there was any danger," Cindy choked out.

"We know," her father assured her. "We know."

"I just wanted to prove I was as good a detective as Nancy, and then, and then—"

"Shhh, Cindy," Terence Austin said, meeting Nancy's gaze over the top of his daughter's h "We understand."

"Nancy saved me." Cindy's voice wa

147

but the words kept pouring out. "She found me and she rescued me."

Terence reached out and soberly shook Nancy's hand. "We owe you so much. How can we ever repay you?"

"It's Cindy who should be congratulated. She has the makings of a good detective. And she's the one who tackled the Master," Nancy replied with a grin.

"Oh, no!" Cindy shook her head. "I'm through with detective work forever. When I finish school, I'm going to choose an easier profession —like brain surgery, or biochemical research!"

Barbara, Terence, and Nancy all laughed. Cindy smiled shyly. She—and her parents— looked happier than Nancy had ever seen them.

Nancy felt a hand drop on her shoulder. She turned to see Ned standing beside her. He was covered with mud. "What happened?" she asked.

"I tackled the Master's friend. Looks like my wardrobe matches yours now." Then he gave her a long look, holding her at arm's length. "What are you wearing?" he demanded.

Nancy laughed and twirled in front of him. "Like it?"

"It's terrible. Especially since Chatham Central's winning!"

Squeezing his arm, Nancy said, "Don't go away. I'll find Chris and change. Then I'll be right back. We can still watch the end of the game together."

Fifteen minutes later Nancy sat beside Ned on the River Heights side of the stadium. Bess and George had found them and were seated one row below. Everyone was interested in hearing about Nancy's daring rescue of Cindy. When she had finished relating the details, George remarked, "Just another day in the life of Nancy Drew, right?"

"That's right," Ned said absently, his eyes on the clock. "Only one minute left until the end of the game, and Chatham Central's still ahead."

Nancy glanced at the field. "Yes, but with one more touchdown and extra point we could still tie. And we've got the ball."

"If the quarterback can ever figure out what to do with it," Ned muttered.

As if hearing him, the River Heights quarterback suddenly threw the football to one of the running backs. The running back dodged and twisted, fighting off the grasping Chatham Central linemen.

Then suddenly the River Heights running back was free—and charging toward the goal line. Nancy and her friends surged to their feet, jumping up and down and screaming.

"He's over!" Ned yelled. "Touchdown!"

The River Heights crowd went wild. The kicker sent the football spinning through the goalposts. "It's a tie!" George cried as the clock ran out. "We did it!"

Bess was cheering loudly. "It's okay that it's a tie! I don't care."

Nancy grinned. "Neither do I. Because we beat the Master."

"The score's wrong," Ned suddenly said.

"What?" Nancy demanded, staring hard at the scoreboard. It read 28–28. She regarded Ned with puzzled eyes.

Ned smiled. "It should be Nancy Drew one, the Master zero."

Nancy slipped her arm through his. She was glad everything had turned out right. The Cindy Austin case was closed and the River Heights team had met Chatham Central's challenge.

"It just takes teamwork," Nancy said. "That's all."

NANCY DREW® MYSTERY STORIES By Carolyn Keene

THE TRIPLE HOAX—#57	69153	$3.50	_____
THE FLYING SAUCER MYSTERY—#58	65796	$3.50	_____
THE SECRET IN THE OLD LACE—#59	69067	$3.50	_____
THE GREEK SYMBOL MYSTERY—#60	67457	$3.50	_____
THE SWAMI'S RING—#61	62467	$3.50	_____
THE KACHINA DOLL MYSTERY—#62	67220	$3.50	_____
THE TWIN DILEMMA—#63	67301	$3.50	_____
CAPTIVE WITNESS—#64	62469	$3.50	_____
MYSTERY OF THE WINGED LION—#65	62681	$3.50	_____
RACE AGAINST TIME—#66	69485	$3.50	_____
THE SINISTER OMEN—#67	62471	$3.50	_____
THE ELUSIVE HEIRESS—#68	62478	$3.50	_____
CLUE IN THE ANCIENT DISGUISE—#69	64279	$3.50	_____
THE BROKEN ANCHOR—#70	62481	$3.50	_____
THE SILVER COBWEB—#71	62470	$3.50	_____
THE HAUNTED CAROUSEL—#72	66227	$3.50	_____
ENEMY MATCH—#73	64283	$3.50	_____
MYSTERIOUS IMAGE—#74	69401	$3.50	_____
THE EMERALD-EYED CAT MYSTERY—#75	64282	$3.50	_____
THE ESKIMO'S SECRET—#76	62468	$3.50	_____
THE BLUEBEARD ROOM—#77	66857	$3.50	_____
THE PHANTOM OF VENICE—#78	66230	$3.50	_____
THE DOUBLE HORROR OF FENLEY PLACE—#79	64387	$3.50	_____
THE CASE OF THE DISAPPEARING DIAMONDS—#80	64896	$3.50	_____
MARDI GRAS MYSTERY—#81	64961	$3.50	_____
THE CLUE IN THE CAMERA—#82	64962	$3.50	_____
THE CASE OF THE VANISHING VEIL—#83	63413	$3.50	_____
THE JOKER'S REVENGE—#84	63426	$3.50	_____
THE SECRET OF SHADY GLEN—#85	63416	$3.50	_____
THE MYSTERY OF MISTY CANYON—#86	63417	$3.50	_____
THE CASE OF THE RISING STARS—#87	66312	$3.50	_____
THE SEARCH FOR CINDY AUSTIN—#88	66313	$3.50	_____
THE CASE OF THE DISAPPEARING DEEJAY—#89	66314	$3.50	_____
THE PUZZLE AT PINEVIEW SCHOOL—#90	66315	$3.95	_____
THE GIRL WHO COULDN'T REMEMBER—#91	66316	$3.50	_____
THE GHOST OF CRAVEN COVE—#92	66317	$3.50	_____
THE SAFECRACKER'S SECRET—#93	66318	$3.50	_____
THE PICTURE PERFECT MYSTERY—#94	66311	$3.50	_____
NANCY DREW® GHOST STORIES—#1	46468	$3.50	_____

and don't forget...THE HARDY BOYS® Now available in paperback

Simon & Schuster, Mail Order Dept. ND5
200 Old Tappan Road, Old Tappan, NJ 07675
Please send me copies of the books checked. (If not completely satisfied, return for full refund in 14 days.)

☐ Enclosed full amount per copy with this coupon
(Send check or money order only.)
Please be sure to include proper postage and handling:
95¢—first copy
50¢—each additonal copy ordered.

☐ If order is for $10.00 or more,
you may charge to one of the
following accounts:
☐ Mastercard ☐ Visa

Name _____ Credit Card No. _____

Address _____

City _____ Card Expiration Date _____

State _____ Zip _____ Signature _____

Books listed are also available at your local bookstore. Prices are subject to change without notice. NDD-25